PRIORS

PRIORS

stories

Marcel Jolley

Black Lawrence Press

BLACK LAWRENCE PRESS
An imprint of Dzanc Books.

Grateful appreciation is made to the publications in which the following stories first appeared: "Priors" *The Portland Review*, Issue 56, Vol. 2 Fall/Winter 2009; "Exchange Rates" *Weber: The Contemporary West*, Vol. 27, No. 1 Fall 2010; "Peripherals" *Interstice*, Vol. 7 2011

Jim Harrison, excerpt "The Theory & Practice of Rivers" from *The Shape of the Journey: New & Collected Poems*. Copyright (c) 1985, 1998 by Jim Harrison. Reprinted with the permission of Copper Canyon Press, www.coppercanyonpress.org

www.blacklawrencepress.com

Executive Editor: Diane Goettel

Book design by Steven Seighman

ISBN: 978-1-936873-19-7

First edition: March 2012

Printed in the United States of America

10 9 8 7 6 5 4 3 2 1

CONTENTS

For my hometown

The days are stacked against
what we think we are.
—Jim Harrison, *The Theory & Practice of Rivers*

PRIORS

PERIPHERALS

During the summer we both turned nine, Eric Lyberg destroyed my right eye and tied our lives together up until he departed this world last Saturday. Because neither of us left the small northern city where we grew up and still had to nod passing hellos, Eric and I were never allowed to become true strangers. Just as certainly, we weren't friends. If life were the job it so often feels like, you might call us coworkers. Not without history, but always professional.

When I saw Eric running east along Glacier Avenue near the Breakwater Inn that Thursday, pulling over to ask if he needed a ride seemed like the right thing to do. In jeans and boots better suited for kicking down doors than jogging, I didn't recognize him at first and almost drove past. He looked like someone much younger. Though many of our generation now exercise to minimize the years, Eric's undisciplined strides suggested an urgency most men have already outrun by the age of forty-one.

Eric flinched at my slowing Explorer, preparing to make for some bordering spruce trees, but then recognized me and was in the passenger seat before I could finish a proper offer.

"Jesus, it's good to see you." He looked directly into my good left eye, the way he had since wrecking the other one. I always appreciated this, as most people bounce between the operative and the prosthetic before finally settling undue attention on the bridge of my nose.

My question of where he was headed received a shrug.

"Y'know, just out and about."

So I simply drove. September showers had been rattling around the Gastineau Channel all day and Eric's soaked denim jacket raised beads of perspiration on my heated seats. He asked how was my state job and the family and I said good on both counts, explaining that Linda had left today with the boys for a weekend cross-country meet in Wrangell. Any inquiries about his life or his family would have required him to regurgitate things I already knew via rumors and police reports published in the *Juneau Empire*. Eric hadn't put out anyone's eye since mine, but most folks would have kept on driving.

"I was planning on hitting McDonald's on the way home for dinner," I said. "Bachelor food, right? What do you say? My treat."

His eyes ricocheted between the Explorer's interior and the lanes around us as another curtain of drizzle overtook Egan Drive.

"Sure," he said. "Can't turn down an offer like that."

And that is how we came to share a bagged dinner at my home, where—by invitation—Eric Lyberg laid low for the next day and a half. We never discussed or even broached the subject of what trouble had started him running. He never asked for the three hundred and eighteen dollars I gave him, and perhaps I was naïve or pretentious to think Eric's problems could be solved by what money I could scrape together without Linda noticing. Though I knew plenty of people, this was the first time I had felt like anyone's friend in quite a while. This went beyond professional courtesy.

———

I can't help but wonder if the incident with my eye was a harbinger of Eric's life to come or the point at which everything swung in that direction. My parents forgave his family but often grumbled about the Lyberg boy being headed down a hard road. Eric wasn't pointing himself down that road, I would think to myself by never say aloud. He wasn't steering at all.

The accident itself—and it truly was accidental—bore that same haphazardness. A group of us had biked across the JD Bridge to Sandy Beach where some pale junior high smokers occupied the lone shelter, forcing us down to the driftwood piles for a round of stickfight—I won't insult anyone's intelligence with an explanation of the rules. Eric Lyberg, until then only an incidental classmate, landed what on any other occasion would have been a dream hit. The water-softened piece of spruce exploded dramatically against my cheekbone, save for a tight knot that punctured and drained my right eye. Even then, Eric took most of the impact. He crumpled to the ground and began shaking his head and crying while other boys yelled pointless warnings about no headshots. One of the girls above us dropped her cigarette and began to puke. All this left me to simply walk a serpentine path in the sand, feeling an odd absence of pressure while a liquid thinner than blood ran down my cheek. The world was now—and would always be—half the size I had known before.

Flying me to the doctors down in Seattle would have been a waste of money, and the summer passed in a collage of bandages, get-well cards and ocular specialists visiting from Anchorage. By the time school started my bruised dark half was learning its dimensions and I knew whatever life was going to throw at me would come from the right. Though possibly mere coincidence, for the next nine years this was where Eric Lyberg chose to sit during our shared classes—in my blind spot. I always sensed he was there, though, and he was. Whenever upperclassmen were giving me shit about my goggle eye or I wanted some beer for the upcoming weekend, Eric waited in the shadows ready to help. Juneau has no roads out and despite holding the obscure and questionable title of longest state capital, it is also the narrowest, dropping to little more than two lanes wide in places where the road clings to a thin shoreline at the base of the mountains. Eric and I could never be more than forty-odd miles apart, and were bound to bump elbows or make eye contact in the tighter spots.

Attending Gonzaga Law after UAS was my only honest effort to break free, but I married a girl from Sitka who'd been bitten by the Outside during a stint at Western Washington University and saw Juneau's theaters and fast food and anemic mall as suitable middle ground. I cannot claim our return was an unhappy one. My job with the State Attorney General's office is challenging and grants me as much prestige as someone who wears a tie can hope to earn in this city.

I have to think Eric made his own escape attempts. There were long stretches of time when he was absent, but I only noticed he was gone in the same way that you don't feel the weather turning until the jacket you wore all summer no longer keeps you warm. Then we would cross paths again—he might be delivering a neighbor's new appliance, or maybe we were both at the Breeze In buying doughnuts. Eric's face would bear a new bruise, his smile inevitably missing yet another tooth, but he never failed to assure me that things were looking up.

My mother was first to call with the news of Eric's death, and several high school acquaintances followed suit over the course of that Sunday afternoon. Linda and the boys were freshly home and unpacking so I took the phone into the cluttered space we originally deemed my study but now call the computer room. Where Mom said *suicide* the others said *lethal combination* but the phone lines swelled with implications. Everyone threw around cop show claptrap like "mainlining" and "hot dose" as if we weren't people with 401k's and Costco memberships and nothing stronger than some expired 222's in our medicine cabinets. No such verbal posturing was present when Eric's younger brother Mark called soon after to ask if I would be a pallbearer that coming weekend.

"He considered you a friend," Mark said. "It would have meant a lot to him."

How could I not agree? Mark thanked me and offered an unprovoked review of his brother's last week alive. There had been recent run-ins with what he called Juneau's shadier elements and another vague incident that had the police looking for Eric, but even Mark could admit that it had just been the combined weight of forty-one years that pushed the needle into his brother's arm and left him to be found on that long weathered staircase climbing a hill near the Governor's mansion. Most passersby assumed him drunk or asleep until some kids noticed frozen vomit.

Aside from mandatory interest in finding Eric's supplier, the police weren't really looking into the affair and Mark assumed the mystery of his brother's last forty-eight hours was probably best unsolved. Even over the phone I could sense him staring at me, right into my good eye. I hadn't seen Mark in years but knew about his own scrapes and time in Lemon Creek before turning into one of those whiplash Christians whom too much early fun has damned to a life of eternal seriousness. I told myself his stare would not be searching for any particular sin, just the ones he knew lay behind everyone's eyes.

"I'll be there," I said before hanging up. "And thanks for thinking of me."

I rejoined Linda and the boys in the living room, where only a few nights earlier Eric and I ate bulk corn tortilla chips and drank a two-liter of store-brand cola while watching a TBS block of John Hughes movies from our youth. The versions were edited but the truly funny parts still carried through. I wondered if Eric also felt tricked by these films and their images of high school and growing up that hadn't meshed with our six hours of direct sunlight and ankle-deep slush. I neglected to ask and we didn't say much. An innocent evening, really, and that afternoon I honestly felt no guilt for not mentioning it to Mark.

My oldest noticed me and despite my grin asked if I was okay. I told them someone I knew had died. Linda covered her mouth and my youngest asked "A friend?"

"Someone I've known a long time," I said.

I was eighteen before giving up hope on the implied consolation prize for losing a sensory organ—a heightening of some other faculty. I waited, expecting one day to hear more or smell more or somehow taste more. Nothing. Maybe this was due to only losing partial vision, though my remaining eye even failed to step up and by twenty-four needed a contact lens to do its job.

If I was disappointed I still never felt gypped or short-changed. Many of the things my Cyclops status disqualified me from or put me at a disadvantage for would have been a challenge with both eyes. By nine I had shown no athletic inclinations, but now any time I was forced onto some curriculum-required playing field or court the bar was set so low I couldn't help but exceed expectations. I was allowed to avoid organized team sports without derision or mockery, and the coaches for the solitary activities I went out for—swimming, cross country and such—attempted to concurrently treat me no different but still cut me some slack. The beautiful Sitka Blacktail I shot at sixteen on Admiralty Island, where my father had dragged me along as a glorified pack mule, was pure luck and a godsend. I think I even closed my good eye before pulling the .308's trigger, but the bullet found the buck square in the shoulder and he still hangs in my father's den as equal parts miracle and assurance that I will never have to go hunting again. My bookish pursuits weren't questioned and dating expectations were so reduced that when I landed Linda as an undergrad no one could believe the luck, myself most of all. I was never expected to throw a game-winning pass or become a jet fighter pilot or a hundred other things that two-eyed boys were capable of but would have to face the inevitable disappointment of not doing.

I won't go so far as to call my injury a "Get Out Of Jail Free" card, but can admit that Eric Lyberg's throw saved me a lot of heartache and hassle. Whether any of this was worth a full field of vision I don't know, but most of the time I'm sure I see more than enough anyway. Regardless, I never found the right time or place to thank him for any of this, and now I guess I never will.

I am the lone pallbearer in a full suit and the only one besides Mark who doesn't take a cigarette when offered. Even he hesitates—if ever there was a time for relapse this is it—but in the end says no thanks. The six of us stand outside the church on a wet fall day that has been judged too temperamental for prolonged lingering around a gravesite, so the small crowd is inside paying last respects to Eric's casket and his parents. The priest has vowed to collect us when the time for our duties arrives.

Most of the other pallbearers are in their nicest jeans and button-up good shirts that only come out on bad occasions. Several I recognize as fellow JDHS grads within four years of myself, and we stare at the sidewalk and speak in clipped exchanges until I am jealous of their addiction, wishing I had something to keep my hands and mouth busy.

"I thought this time it might work."

This from a man I remember only as once having been led from metal shop class by the principal and a police officer. Everyone agrees in puffs but only Mark—perhaps just for lack of a cigarette—speaks up.

"You all did what you were supposed to," he says. "But it wasn't ever up to us."

Again a round of agreement, and I can sense their shared undertone of satisfaction in knowing that this idiot, his expensive suit soaking in all their smoke, is on the outside. Only after the group disbands into smaller clusters along the sidewalk does Mark pull me aside and explain how this time was supposed to have been different.

These people had been Eric's support structure, offering decades of couches to crash on and small loans they knew would settle nothing, would never be returned. They had posted bail and stood as character witnesses and driven across our long skinny town to pick Eric up when life left him beyond walking distance from home. They were his friends.

"So when the cops started snooping around for him, I called everyone I knew," Mark says. "We all agreed—no more handouts, no more help."

A deep breath says his separation from nicotine has been short and hard.

"We knew that Eric getting hauled in, maybe some honest time with a state-mandated rehab program, was what he really needed," Mark says. "Everyone who cared about him promised to call the cops if he showed up. It was the only thing that could have saved him."

The priest's head emerges. He uses only his eyes and brow to indicate that our time is approaching. Marlboro 100's are tossed on damp pavement and crushed beneath uncomfortable dress shoes.

"We thought we'd covered all the bases," Mark says. "Eric

had burned most of his other bridges. But somehow he got more. Got enough. Who knows where from."

His hand is on my shoulder, guiding me back into the church. He is comfortable with the role and I let him lead me.

"This isn't the town we grew up in anymore, is it?" Mark says.

Inside wait three pews full of people who could probably tell me if three-hundred and eighteen dollars could result in this. But even a lame dud like me who only tried pot twice in high school knows the answer. Eric likely died with walking-around money in his pocket. Linda hasn't noticed the cash missing and never will.

My hands start shaking as I take my place at the rear right. Smart positioning, as this is the only station allowing me a view of all the other pallbearers. But I don't really need to see them, because finally, thirty-two years after the fact, my reward is here. I hear everything. I can hear everything these men have said in the last few days, everything they promised to band together for, everything they will do to the person who visited this upon their friend. I can hear what they are thinking and the silent psalm tremoring across Mark's stiff lip. I hear it all.

The six of us share a glance when we first lift Eric from the stand. He is lighter than anyone expected. But looking around this church full of men and women I've partially known my entire life, this is no surprise. Everyone here, myself included, looks too fat or too skinny or too old—different from how we remember each other. Maybe this world allows some people to pass through perfect and unchanged, but not anyone I know.

HOOD RIVER

I am looking for the face my father was willing to die for. The Amtrak Coast Starlight she was scheduled to arrive on idles at the platform outside with an occasional air-brake sigh, and I scan Portland's anachronistic Union Station for a face I don't know. Technically, I have seen her—in our e-mail correspondence she included a link to her Facebook page, though I will be hard-pressed to place her if not flanked by friends and alcohol in a skin-blasting flash or viewed from an arm's length looking upward thoughtfully. I know she enjoys any books she can get her hands on, loves *Donny Darko* and *The Breakfast Club* and every cult classic in between, and wants me to kill my television save for *The Daily Show* and *Scrubs*. Not much to work with, but to access more photos and her blog would have required my joining something, an activity that at thirty-eight I am increasingly reluctant to do.

She has no idea what I look like, and physical resemblances to my father are minimal. By my age all his teeth were lost to causes ranging from bar fights to workplace mishaps. His hair remained a charming collection of dark cowlicks where mine is greying but manageable. Despite dentures, Dad always smiled like he had just found a twenty in his pocket, whereas my ex-wife pinpointed my snapshot grin, the one I wear now, as "waiting for impact."

When my phone rings I hope for an unidentified number, maybe saying she got off the train in Seattle and forgot to get back on or she's just not coming at all. Instead a deceptively innocent *Mom* illuminates the screen.

"Is she there?"

"Not yet, Mom. Her train just arrived."

"And how will you recognize her?"

I should just say *pictures* but for some reason try to explain Facebook.

"Be careful," she says. "I've seen a show where men your age get arrested for things like that."

"She's twenty-three."

"And a train? Really?" She pauses for a sip of something for which the hour is probably too early. "What does she look like?"

At twenty-three my mom had a six-month-old me underfoot and an accidental husband taking whatever seasonal job kept him away the most. How do I describe this twenty-three without breaking sixty-one's heart?

"Normal," I say. "Nothing special, just a normal-looking girl."

"That figures. He spends his life chasing women out of his league and cashes out for a normal one. I hope it doesn't sound bitchy but I'm glad I didn't come along."

"I understand." Her coming would have been the ultimate act of bitchiness. My mother remarried quite well twenty years ago to a commercial real estate manager in Bellingham named Chester. I have otherwise only known pets named Chester but we get on fine and he's given my mother a beautiful home on Chuckanut Bay where I imagine her studying the water as we speak.

And then before me is a normal girl. The normal girl.

"Mom, I have to go."

"Watch out," I hear her say. "She might be after something."

Like what? I want to ask, but she is gone.

"Sarah?"

She laughs. "I knew it was you."

I check my hair and instinctively want to call for a dental cleaning. She points to my hand holding the phone, zeroing in on the space where my left pinky finger should be.

"He told you about that?"

"Sam talked about you a lot," she said. "I guess he was proud."

I don't ask if he mentioned any schooling or sports achievements or merit badges—all these paled beside a deck incident that guaranteed I would never be more than a rhythm guitarist reliant on bar chords, unable to ever again truly hang loose. Sarah has only a shoulder satchel and at her feet a large brown duffel, as carelessly jammed and ambiguous as she is in cargo pants and a hooded ROOTS sweatshirt.

"And you have...him?"

She pats the duffel. "Right in here. You should've seen the looks from the TSA in Anchorage."

Maybe I actually expected her to carry my father's remains into the terminal like a scepter or idol held overhead, but I can't help thinking he's just as happy stuck in there with her underthings and iPod.

"Anything else?"

"Nope," she says. "Jammin' econo, right?"

I agree with a glance at the floor and we head to my beige four-door Saturn.

"So how long a drive are we looking at?" she says, pulling out her iPhone.

"Just an hour or so," I say. "We can get something to eat first. Something fast."

"Fast is good." She chuckles at whatever the screen says and her fingers set to work in that way my twelve-year-old assures me is rude to interrupt. I am almost to 405 North when she looks up.

"I've heard Portland is cool," she says after a two-block study.

"This is the Pearl District," I say. "It was designed to look cool."

She approves. "And you live here? The Pearl? Or not?"

This comes with a glance encompassing the Saturn, which my ex still calls the permanent rental car. I confirm that I do not.

"That's okay." She cranes at yet another bento or sushi place. "Not everyone can live in these places, right? That's what makes them cool."

Both my parents used to joke—without laughing—that I ruined a great summer fling. They met in Juneau, where for reasons still unclear to me my mother had come north for the summer after graduating from Eastern Washington State College in Cheney. My dad was longshoring and working boats here and there. In addition to having undeniable charms, he swooned my mother with his ability to get the previous week's *Seattle P-I*, which he bought from barge deckhands for triple the face value. They fell into one of those loves that survive only in the extended daylight of a high latitude summer, heading north in September on a bundle of cash to see a little country. They only made Whitehorse, Yukon before my mom discovered she was pregnant. They were married by the magistrate in Haines the next week. For the better part of ten years—and too many schools to count—my mother was able to deny the obvious before heading off on the course that ended with Chester and Chuckanut Bay. As far as I can tell, my dad managed to maintain this denial right up until a week ago.

Dad often played the word *wanderlust* like a trump card, wandering away so much more often than he wandered home. He grew up in Hood River, Oregon, watching the dams choke off wild salmon runs and admiring the river barges drifting west, ready to mimic all that water's course at his first legal chance. His last job before heading north at eighteen was with a private security company entrusted to guard Cold War secrets at the Hanford nuclear site near the Tri-Cities. They—the government, he claimed—had given him a small blue capsule, which for as long as I can remember hung attached to his keys by a small wire. Cyanide, Sam told everyone, to kill himself with should he ever be taken hostage and interrogated. He admitted to never having paid enough attention to learn anything worth even his life, but when drinking he often pulled the capsule out to roll between his fingers.

"Just in case," he would say.

I received the phone call at two a.m. last Saturday. It was an Anchorage doctor, regretting to inform me that my father was dead from acute hypothermia. A crab boat had overturned on the western extremities of Bristol Bay and left Sam and his crewmates floating for the better part of the night in their covered life raft. My father gave his survival suit to a female crewmember who had failed to get her own from the sinking vessel. Even with the late hour and third-hand retelling of the story, I recognized Dad's odd feeling of immortality and—Sarah being female—suspected ulterior motives. He had sat hip-deep in the icy waters seeping into the raft until the Coast Guard found them, and was joking around right up until he died in the chopper on the way back to Kodiak. The doctor heaped posthumous praise onto my father, both personal and passed on by his crewmates, but I wasn't really listening. Even while arranging for Sam's cremation, organizing Sarah's trip and making plans to scatter his ashes in Hood River, one thought stayed with me. I just kept wondering what happened to his little blue capsule.

At a Gresham AMPM mini-market, Sarah collects a large fountain drink, an angry cylinder promising energy, one bag of Ruffles and a cellophane whip containing either licorice or something meat-based. Some honest fat peeks over her waistband and a second chin pops out with certain expressions, but I am jealous of what I hope is her authentic indifference. She is through most of a Clif Bar when we reach the counter, where she deposits the empty wrapper with the rest of her take next to my Diet Snapple and Nature Valley Bar. My twenty covers everything and she leaves the wrapper for the clerk to throw away.

Back on 84 East she asks what I do. Having yet to find anyone interested in the intricacies of maintenance programs for a regional airline, I offer my standard.

"I'm in aircraft maintenance. Mainly the paperwork side."

"Sounds okay," she says. "Must be or you wouldn't do it, right?"

"It can be okay, most times."

"Or if it isn't okay, you've at least come to terms with that and accept it as a necessary evil—I mean, it seems that's what the options are." She pulls a long draw of soda. "And you can just drop things in the middle of the week, that's nice."

Again, I could fill ten minutes with the advantages of user time as opposed to old-fashioned sick time and how the policy favors those who stay healthy, but simplicity seems best.

"There's flexibility." I look to her duffel in the back seat. "For circumstances. So how you did you end up in Kodiak? Are you from there?"

A mid-sip chuckle escapes down the straw into her soda.

"No, but I should punch you for thinking I could be," she says. "Officially I'm from Clovis, but I went to Humboldt State and I'm headed back to live with some friends in Eureka, so pretty soon I'll be able to say I'm from there." The cellophane whip reveals meat and she pushes words around a chunk she bites off. "The whole fishing thing was kind of a lark. I wanted something real, something extreme, y'know? And I saw that show *Deadliest Catch*, and it just looked so intense. I asked my folks for a ticket north after graduation and off I went."

"Had you worked on boats before?"

Her head shake is a boast. "Nope. Just hung out in the bars, talked to some skippers. I was actually hired as a cook—in school I cooked for our house with like eight people living there, so I was legit. I was learning the deck stuff, but then, y'know..."

She glances at her bag, which I still have no proof contains my father.

"I saw them, though—the *Deadliest Catch* crew? They mostly follow the boats from Dutch Harbor, but I saw them filming around St. Paul and was hoping they'd want to talk to me—the whole female in a boys' club angle—but they were busy. I just think it'd be cool to be on there, to have the season's DVD as proof and all to show friends, and kids if that ever happens. Who knows, they might follow up with everything that went down. I left them all my contact info."

"But you're doing okay?"

Her nod comes slow and thoughtful, a cynic might say rehearsed.

"Yeah, I'm hanging in there, working through things. That's one reason I'm headed to Eureka. Surround myself with friends, their energy. It's a pretty intense deal, but like my friend Buggy told me, I have to think I lived for a reason. Back on that horse or whatever they say about the deep end of the pool."

When I ask if she plans on returning to the sea, Sarah stops an exaggerated laugh with her mouth in mid-gape.

"I think that box is checked, don't you?"

Her therapeutic travel options included several friends kicking around Prague, others teaching English in Bali, or there's always backpacking in Chile. All things, Sarah attests, she will accomplish before stepping onto the grid, if she chooses to do so at all. The locations play through my brain like magazine snapshots that even I recognize as oversimplified stereotypes. I've travelled less than one would assume with my airline benefits and when I do any enjoyment springs more from the universalities revealed than any novelty. If I am jealous it is only for the further proof Sarah will have of the world's flatness and uniformity.

"So Sam as a dad," she says as we pass Troutdale and the Cascades start to stand at attention. "That had to be a trip."

Where to start? Birthday cards arriving at least three weeks late with a wrinkled fifty and scrawled *love, Pop*. Being able to tell my schoolmates my father was somewhere on the ocean while their own soft-bellied dads toiled away behind ties and desks. Every reunion beginning with an exclamation of how I've grown and laughing hugs that threatened to bruise. Mere weeks later he would begin checking the calendar, revealing that old eagerness to leave. My young mother would wait until I was watching TV and she had started the washing machine to allow herself to cry.

"It was interesting," I say. "I think he had trouble deciding whether his seasonal job was fishing or family."

"I can't imagine Sam married," Sarah says.

"It was a challenge for him, too."

"What was she like?"

"She's still alive," I say, though for some reason I don't think Sarah assumes my mother dead, but merely past tense. "They were just different. They never belonged together."

"But doesn't that mean you shouldn't be here?"

An artificial digital scale fills my Saturn, and the iPhone is in her hand like a quick-draw artist's pistol. She marvels at the reception despite the Gorge's encroaching walls and explains our plans to someone in clipped tones.

"No, he's cool," she says, and only acknowledges me after a few miles with an estimating glance equal parts indifference and uncertainty.

"I don't know. Forty, probably."

I consider correcting her, getting back those two important years, but realize she will be right soon enough.

I distinctly remember seeing the tanker truck that would skid and then erupt into flames, closing 84 West. The rig passed us in the opposite lanes just outside Hood River and appeared as a rope of smoke in my rear view shortly thereafter as emergency equipment howled by. I can't help but wonder by exactly what margin we missed seeing that particular accident, maybe being part of it.

By the time we ease off the exit I can see Oregon State Troopers rerouting westbound traffic over the bridge to the two anemic lanes of Washington's Highway 14 on the Columbia's north bank. Already Dad will cost me a seventy-five cent toll on top of the snacks necessary to keep Sarah running. She is anchoring several concurrent communications and I'm getting the leftovers from intermittent calls and texting. Only as we pull onto Hood River's main drag—outdoor stores holding hands with coffee shops and stylish eateries, all engineered to appear a casual accident—does she look up with approval.

"Nice." She taps a last rebuttal and pockets the iPhone. "You ever been to Telluride? Or Crested Butte?"

I barely fit in two *no*'s before she continues.

"Same groove. So this is where Sam grew up."

"This is where he's from," I say. "Geographically. He was gone before a lot of this, back when the wind was an annoyance rather than an attraction."

I want to know more about this place that produced my father, to have anecdotes for street names and buildings and businesses. Like too many things I know only through Sam's stories, the dimensions don't match and I find myself *turned around*, that soft modern descendent of *lost*. Somewhere hides the healthy stream that ran clear and pinprick cold behind my grandfather's musty house down from Mount Hood into the Columbia and on to the Pacific. Sam's trips home became solo affairs after my eleventh year, when bringing a kid into the bar stopped being cute and even he recognized leaving me in the car as irresponsible. I blame this gap for my inability to locate the stream. Instead of my grandfather's place we find only newly-sprouted wood homes whose gates and *Protected by ADT* signs hardly invite expeditions for whatever water may or may not run behind their property. Sarah remains unfazed.

"A beer, maybe?"

The brew pub downtown simmers with talk of the accident on 84 and rain in the Gorge slowing the winding Highway 14 detour. A few patrons walk to the corner where they can look down on the river and confirm that the peristaltic backup now extends onto the bridge. The bar TV shows some junior reporter on the scene with a hand to his ear confirming all routes out of the Gorge are clogged. An honest grey drizzle darkens the pavement outside, and I envision scattered ashes congealing into something like wet paper maché paste.

"So you want to spread him in that creek?" Sarah says.

"That was the idea."

"Why don't you just ask someone where it's at?"

"I don't know the name," I say. "Or if it even had a name. There are so many streams here. It doesn't have to be that one, it was just my plan."

"Maybe it's Sam's revenge," Sarah says. "He never seemed big on plans."

My look—asking how much she could learn about my father in a month and why I might be the deserving target of any revenge—ricochets off the two dark pints the bartender delivers. Sarah digs into her nearby bag, emerging not with money but a silver cylinder that I've only seen before on the Anchorage crematorium's website. In person the urn looks less like a seamless space-age vessel and more like a standby hydraulic reservoir from one of my airline's turboprops.

"How about a round on the house?"

All earth tones and sparse facial hair, the bartender doesn't smile. "Is that a bomb?"

"Depends," Sarah says. "How many rounds is a bomb good for?"

This death-threat flirting comes natural to the sturdy Sarah, but unsettles our bony bartender's footing like a freshman's first bench press.

"It's an urn," I say.

The bartender says okay but appeared more comfortable with the bomb.

"So it's full of ashes?"

"Cremains." Sarah grins. "Isn't that a great word? It's his father, we're here to scatter him. I was there, y'know, when he died."

"No shit? That's heavy."

Sarah agrees through her first sip. "Yeah, but you deal." She puts a hand atop Sam. "So what do you say?"

"Yeah, I guess." A quick glance around offers him no guidance. "You probably should get him off the bar. Health codes and all." His eyes meet mine in a passing flash. "Condolences, man."

Instead of returning him to her bag Sarah places my father on the floor between our barstools. I offer a toast, for one last round on Sam. Her already half-empty glass offers a clink distinct from my own.

"So what's the plan now?"

Again I look at the rain, which now has a little momentum at its back. "Well, I suppose the river will be just fine, I can try to pick a good spot." I imagine waiting for a westbound barge to pass, giving Dad one last chance to hitch a ride downstream. "It's already two-fifty, though, and that accident is a real monkey wrench. With your flight tonight we should probably just head back now."

"I'm not going to rush you," Sarah says. "And there's always another flight. I can rebook for tomorrow."

"Maybe I could spend the night," I say. "Get up early after this weather has blown through and start fresh. There's a Greyhound station here. I'll buy you a ticket to meet up with your plane in Portland."

Sarah finishes her pint. "No way. I've got everything I own in my bags, I'm all set for an overnight."

"Really, you've gone above and beyond already."

"Hey, we're in this adventure together, right?"

Her hand falls on mine and she smiles in a way that the world hasn't yet had a chance to carve that charming fat from, and then I am in that raft seeing what Sam saw.

Though I suspect proper adventures don't start on rainy Tuesdays at three p.m., I leave Sarah, Sam and one of my credit cards at the bar in search of lodging. The motel I find is nearby and so clean the clerk appears to think twice upon seeing my missing digit, unsure if I am trustworthy clientele. I leave the car and on the walk back to the bar call my supervisor to say I'll be in tomorrow afternoon—this is fine, of course, as my work is of even less urgency than interest—and then call my ex-wife. There is no real reason—I don't pick Trevor up until Friday and our next tentative nuclear family get-together isn't until a week from Saturday. I call because she will answer. We do not hate or even dislike each other. Though no one ever asks, I present Yvonne and I as simply friends who fell in love until one day we found we'd fallen out. I call because I never know when we might fall back in.

"And you left her there?" Yvonne says after I give her the afternoon's Cliffs Notes. "With the urn? What if she takes off with him?"

Any accusation in her tone is buried beneath a chuckle.

"She's had plenty of chances to do that already," I say. "Besides, I'm paying her bar tab."

"Single king or two queens?"

"Two beds, thank you."

"Hey, don't let me stop you if you're hitting it off."

Crossing the overpass, 84 West below me appears to be moving again and I avert my eyes. I want to stay trapped here, to drink more heavy beer and get my forty-nine dollars of adventure from the motel room.

"I think she's having more fun with a dead Sam than a live me, so we're probably safe."

We? And safe from what? The digital lines sag with weight as Yvonne and I both wait for something to pass.

"But you're okay?" she says. "With everything?"

"I guess. So far so good."

"I just hope all this serves a purpose. For you." Behind her I hear rising the whirlwind of Trevor home from school. "But I also hope you don't expect too much, and you don't end up disappointed somehow."

I nod until I am sure the phone has transferred the gesture to her. "That Trev?"

"Yeah, just a minute."

Then I am out of Hood River and into a world of geography homework, budding social cliques and authoritative injustices. He knows Grandpa Sam is gone but not what I'm doing today, for fear he'd want to come along or think the whole enterprise creepy. After I hang up, promising Trevor a coast trip this weekend if the weather allows and Yvonne a follow-up call upon arriving back in Portland, I am momentarily ashamed both for my lie of omission and for hesitating when offered my choice of beds, wondering what sleepwear Sarah has packed. I am someone's father—but so was Sam.

Sarah is gone from the bar. My extremities burn thinking Yvonne was right and I already fear the call to my mother, explaining how some young skirt in long pants has run off with what was left of her ex-husband. My first thought is the police, though an afternoon of redirecting traffic will find them less than thrilled to help. Maybe I can call Dad's container a bomb, and let the details work themselves out after Sarah is apprehended.

A whistle tears the bar chatter and classic rock cloud down the center, one of those tucked two-fingered call-to-action numbers that people aren't learning to do anymore. Except Sarah—of course she can do this. She waves me back to a corner table where the health codes relax enough to allow Sam to act as centerpiece. Around her sit three young men who are less individuals than different interpretations of the same theme. All are intensely comfortable and dress so much like carpenters they can only be bike store clerks or programmers. Two make room for me with parental welcome and introductions are made. There is a Josh and a Lucas and a Hunter, but I can't guess in which order.

"So Lucas had a great idea," Sarah says, "About Sam."

Lucas, who I'd tagged as Josh, describes the great little stream that feeds the Hood below his parents' condo, complete with an idyllic trail and bridge and everything. Plans are already in place for a get-together later tonight with friends— all good people, I am assured—which could easily segue into an acceptable wake with some drink substitutions and the right mix of music.

"Or we could drive up to the mountain," says the one I had originally assumed to be Lucas. "Or off the top of Beacon Rock. A friend of mine was able to get a copy of the key for the park gate."

Sarah seconds every suggestion. I want to tuck the urn under an arm and Heisman my way back out into the rain.

"Thanks, guys, but I need to mull it over a little more."

"But I think Sam would appreciate the spontaneity," says the man who, by default, is Hunter. "And it sounds like he enjoyed a good party."

Who are these people, and how do they know so much about a man who after thirty-eight years I'm still putting together?

"You're all probably right," I say. "But let's just let him hang at the bar a little longer."

On cue another dark round arrives, flanking a mound of bacon-accented nachos. The beer is icy and I am soon through my first and started on another, fumbling through throwaway conversation lobbed my way because these guys think I can somehow grant access to Sarah. They all turn out to be nothing if not polite and each independently assures me that the whole situation with my dad lies between "really sucks" and "completely sad." I can't tell whether their vocabulary or emotional range is the limiting factor, but the sentiment is appreciated and I listen to slurred tales of their own fathers, all still with us and tucked safely into corner offices or second marriages.

Josh is first to notice my hand. He starts a little but says nothing. To the surgeon's credit the injury can be mistaken for a birth defect, and being downstream from Hanford one never knows. I offer him a closer look and talk about the sliding pots and how no one was really to blame, giving them all license to mutter curses and study my phantom digit. The attention mixes well with my beers, and I'm surprised my accident warrants anything in this den of adrenaline junkies. When they share scar stories I realize they have made sure to get injuries that display well and make good copy but still allow them to type or play piano.

Sarah answers every offering with talk of some worse damage she almost encountered. There is a friend's non-fatal stabbing at the house party in high school, the fellow traveler beaten up outside the Phuket hostel two summers ago, and the game-closer of watching Sam freeze. Her body remains soft and showroom perfect despite this life lived just abeam disaster. My missing finger begins to ache and I tuck my hand back under the table.

My mother's call comes as the muted TV over the bar shows 84 West flowing smoothly. No longer trapped, I'm glad to be too drunk for the drive home. Excusing myself to the street, I answer and Mom asks if the task is done.

"Not really," I say. "We hit a snag."

She huffs at my bullet points of lost streams, closed interstates and last rounds.

"He probably couldn't find that stream himself. Any water flowing somewhere else would probably suit him fine."

"Still, Mom…" I stop, knowing despite the acidic years and big houses on Chuckanut Bay she understands.

"What about the Siren?"

"She's staying, I guess." A glance back inside reveals that the spotlight is back on Sarah and Sam has scooted, I swear, a little closer.

"Do you like her?"

"I don't know," I say. "I suppose I can at least say I see why Dad might have made the choice he did."

"That's doesn't answer my question."

"I love you, Mom. Get some sleep."

"Call me," she says with a rare crack in her voice. "Afterwards. So I know you're okay."

I promise I will and pocket the phone. Before returning inside I soak in a little of the moist night, knowing the rain will return sooner than later.

I knew people treated me different because I was Sam's son. Even when I didn't offer it up the connection always bubbled to the surface.

"So you're Sam's boy," they would say, following with a wink or laugh or eye roll like we were all in on the same joke. No questions or eyebrows rose when I arrived at the store for beer or cigarettes with a scribbled note that Dad assumed was adequate legal speak. People inquiring how the old man was, though if they knew Sam well enough to ask they also knew he would always make out okay. Everyone insisted I tell Dad to call them sometime, despite the fact that they knew he could be found on the couch or downtown if he was ashore. When walking the gravel streets alone I was always offered a ride, and women with whom I was too shy to make eye contact joked about my future with the ladies.

Summers spent with my father in various shore towns regularly left me with the feeling that something was expected of me, something which I realized early on I would be unable to deliver. Maybe the closest I ever came was losing my finger, which had far less to do with heredity and birthrights than just occupational odds. Sam would have laughed and punched my shoulder hard had I used a term like *royalty*, but being his son in a place whose existence rotated around docks and boats was arguably the most special I will ever feel in my life. When I got off that jet down at my mom's I returned to being another kid from a broken home whose grades would earn some partial scholarship to study a safe subject at a state school, so I learned to enjoy those times when by dint of my last name people expected something of me.

An admission I can only make now that Sam is gone: I have never liked beer. Because of advertising I understand the role alcohol is supposed to play—camaraderie, relaxation, freedom—and like tonight, I have done my best to perpetuate this and down my fair share. But no matter how well crafted by brewmasters, the taste always makes my tongue take a fazed step back, and even during the most euphoric effects I know I am in essence poisoning myself and feel—at least in part— preemptively regretful.

A similar aversion is growing for Sarah, and though I wonder if she senses this I am doubtful. Talk in the last hour has turned to Burning Man and Bonnaroo and My Morning Jacket, yet always slingshots around any conversational moon back into Sarah's orbit. She commandeers the three boys' stories with obnoxious lassos like "That sounds like a thing *I* would do," or "That is so *me*." Even if they are unaware, Josh and Lucas and Hunter are just doing their duty in the reproductive cycle—listening, laughing, waiting for their chance to fertilize this strong vessel, which despite all her bombast each of us realizes would give our progeny a stronger than average chance of survival. They are only doing what Sam did in that raft, sacrificing themselves in hopes of being with her. Everything happening around me is very natural, right down to my dad waiting in his can to be reintroduced to the waters from whence he rose. The whole mess is organic and makes total sense when one steps back to take it all in, but this doesn't stop me from not liking her anymore.

"I'm going home." The moment I speak I realize how this sounds like a kid invited only because he owns the football. "I'm just tired, y'know."

Josh adopts what too many afterschool specials have told him is a concerned expression. "No way, man. You're in no shape to drive to Portland."

"Not *home* home," I say. "The motel. To sleep."

He and his friends exchange looks but can find no fault, save for the rug of financial support I am pulling from beneath them.

"It's not even nine," Sarah says.

"I know, but I want to be up early tomorrow. You don't have to stop on my account."

I track down an indifferent server to settle my tab and pull the urn towards me.

"You're taking Sam?" Sarah says. "This night is all about him."

Is it? I think, but just say, "Yeah."

The three suitors look relieved, either at having the cremains off the table or because even dead Sam is too much competition. I slide Sarah's key card across the table and stand, cradling the urn like an award I wasn't favored to win but everyone knew I deserved.

"It's a short walk down the street," I say. "If you need it, I mean."

Sarah says okay but only her face isn't pouting. The rest of her contorts to spell some full-body curse word. The best any of these boys can hope for now is an angry hump that will somehow leave them feeling violated. I am smiling and actually laugh out loud a few blocks away, walking in a moonless rain back from the bar with my dad.

I have always attributed the fundamental disconnect between Sam and I to the fact that I lay on shore. He was not himself without some water under his boots. During our times together whatever house we were in always felt more mine than his, and I never took his readiness to leave personally. The sea was his work and those times I shared a deck with him were different— he was comfortable, our duties as crew members giving him the guidance that was missing as family.

As I grew older people still treated me different. During cold snaps neighbors would check to see if I was okay and make sure I knew how to run the furnace without blowing up the house. When the two twenties left to feed myself until Dad's return didn't cover the groceries I laid on the counter, the clerk was told to put my purchase on a tab that no right-thinking businessman, despite all the winks and backslaps, would ever grant Sam. My future as a lady killer gave way to descriptors like responsible and level-headed. Eventually I fashioned my own year-round life down south, and when I returned on sporadic visits no one even recognized me as Sam's boy.

Sarah's entering wakes me from one of those beer-drunk dreams that moves like a car sliding slowly on snow—a sloppy control is implied and any impact will be marginal. In the dream I am still in Hood River, but joined by Yvonne and Trevor. Sam is already sifted somewhere perfect and the day defies the season. Roads to everywhere are open and running fast but we are in no hurry to leave. I can't remember whether to turn into or out of the skid.

Sarah could've come through the window and been quieter. She is all impact and unwarranted force. My role is to acknowledge, but I instead feign sleep with so little movement she can't mistake the ruse. The TV comes on, Letterman snarking it up with some celebrity too perfect to have anything to offer.

"I always fall asleep to the TV." She drops on her bed and puts the remote on the table between us. "You can turn it off after I'm out."

I agree by rolling over, helmeting myself with a pillow. Minutes pass—tooth brushing, undressing, bag shuffling. My beer dream is off the road and buried to the rims. Best to walk home and tow it out tomorrow.

"Thanks a lot," she says.

"You're welcome."

"No." Her tone is a playground shove. "I mean it."

"Not a problem."

"Real class, ditching me back there with the Three Stooges."

"You appeared to be having fun." I don't surrender my protective pillow. "They seemed like three nice guys, or maybe just the same nice guy."

"Yeah, but I thought we were in this together."

I roll over. Her hair is up and she wears a liberating tank top and shorts that are not athletic or appropriate. Her weaknesses and indulgences can't hide and I am reminded of the beautiful leeway that youth both grants and is granted.

"Then I'm sorry," I say. "But this trip isn't about us."

"And you couldn't have left him there?"

A quick glance assures me Sam is still at the foot of my bed, where I can defend him with a quick kick.

"He shouldn't have been there in the first place," I say. "That felt like a stunt."

Her attention goes to the TV. "I just think I deserve some time with him."

"What about the whole trip down?" Even as I make this insipid argument I imagine fellow Amtrak passengers seeking other cars or even flinging themselves off the train to avoid this selfish bitch wearing my father like a medal. "And that's bullshit, anyway. This isn't about you."

Her stare at the set intensifies, so much I imagine the tube will pop and I wonder how much that will run me at checkout.

"Sam is gone," she says. "This is my story and I'm not going to feel bad about being at the center. Sam's story ended so mine could go on."

Her eyes, slightly too big for her face and tearing up, snap on me.

"That's...do you realize the pressure it puts on me?"

Sitting up, my belly sloshes with heavy alcohol and I'm glad I left a shirt on, sparing the room a view of my soft form.

"You knew my dad, what, maybe a month?"

Sarah nods a reluctant agreement.

"An intense month, though..."

"Sure," I say. "But maybe you noticed how he saw himself. He thought he was..."

I bite back on *invincible*, with the word's images of square chests and capes. Even Sam, in his sagging jeans and hickory shirts, wouldn't go so far.

"…he'd gone in rafts before. He joked about having frequent flyer miles with the Coast Guard."

A shared grin rattles between our beds. Letterman's credits earn me a little more attention.

"I'm just saying that chances are Sam didn't think he was giving anything up with that suit. He probably thought the chopper would be there within an hour and that night he would be a hero with wet jeans."

Sarah hugs her knees up to her chest and rests her chin on them, offering an oblique view of her armpit with only shadows saving her dignity.

"Fuck you."

"What's that for?"

"Fuck you for taking me out of the story."

"That wasn't my intent…"

"No. Fuck you." She slams a pillow and inadvertently brings her right breast into view. She catches me looking but doesn't cover up. "You give me shit for wanting any attention, but you're like a co-star in your own life. And that is worse."

"I know," I say. "I just didn't want you to be weighed down."

The crying hardly seems a precedent and her glances land sporadically on the TV, but she is hurt. Hurt that her life may not have been worth sacrifice, hurt that the whole raft episode was a poorly-planned attempt to get in her pants. She is hurt and afraid that Sam had been the star of his movie and stayed that way right up until everything went black. She will miss the weight I am trying to lift off her the way I miss all those things that were once expected of me as Sam's son.

Any attempt at physical consolation is questionable with her breast still exposed, so I take up the remote and silence the TV. The resultant crackling glow owns the next few minutes.

"I feel like we should fuck," she says.

"That's an option?" The words are out before I can catch them, and I feel doughy, unshowered, needing to take a piss.

"I don't sleep around." She takes this time to readjust herself. "Don't think that. It might just help balance things out."

My mind races through the mechanics—who will move to which bed? What kind of contraception is involved or available in Hood River on a Tuesday after sundown? Where will we place Sam, who seems to hum in his container at the end of the bed? How will this fit into my dream of Yvonne and Trevor and an open road home?

Sarah rolls away in a rustle louder than I would guess possible with cheap sheets. "Never mind."

"No, Sarah. I'm just thinking…"

"Never mind," she says. "Good night."

I say nothing, waiting for her to offer again or demand a response or just start snoring. Headlights stream around the edges of the curtains, the brighter setups of downshifting big rigs making it halfway across the ceiling. I am sober now and the highway sounds clear. Nothing is keeping me in this town.

"You weren't there," she says.

"No. I wasn't."

I emerge from the shower to find Sarah returned from her morning walk with Sam's canister. Our first olive branch had come earlier, when I awoke at 7:13 a.m. to find her slipping Sam into her satchel near the door.

"I just need him for a little while," she said. "For a walk."

To prove no ill will she gestured toward her still unpacked duffel, overflowing with wrinkled clothes and digital errata with which I could console myself should she steal away with Dad. I offered a wave of approving trust and reclosed my eyes.

Sarah now holds a ticket for the Greyhound leaving in forty minutes to take her back into Portland and her flight southbound to Eureka or Prague or Bali or just home. My offer to reimburse the cost gets waved off initially but she still takes the twenty I extend. I tell her I'll be just a few minutes and retreat back into the bathroom, leaving her with morning television.

Soon we are packed and checked out and sitting in front of Hood River's small Greyhound station. We are alone, all other passengers either gone already or giving Hood River a chance for one more day.

"So have you decided what you're going to do?" she says.

I shake my head. "Not really. I'm going to kick around this morning, see if anything or any place strikes me."

She starts to say something but bites back, hesitating a little for my benefit before trying again.

"Thanks for the beer and the food and everything," she says. "I know you probably didn't budget for all that."

"Thanks for the company."

She assures me it was no problem and huffs and says *Well then* in a way confirming we won't hug and I am not to leave the car. We volley a few benign standards—travel safe, stay cool, and so on—and I break protocol by opening my car door, though only to stand and lean, watching until she is inside the building and knowing she will always think I am stupid.

She thought me stupid that morning, assuming I would not follow her. Dressing quickly, I caught up a few blocks away, her ears jammed with headphone buds making my lazy tailing that much easier. I watched her enter the Greyhound station, fully exhaling only when she emerged with the ticket and weighted satchel.

She thinks me stupid for not knowing that the urn beside me now contains only about sixty percent of my father, mixed with baking soda, malted cereal and river sand to return him to an unsuspicious weight and bulk. I saw her come out of the Chevron Food Mart carrying the Arm & Hammer and Malt-O-Meal boxes along with a breakfast burrito and the metal travel thermos into which she poured roughly a third of Sam. This took place at a riverside bench where I estimated about two to three percent of him was lost in the wind that had already picked up despite the early hour. After adding a handful of sand and giving Sam a settling shake, Sarah washed her fingers in an eddy and set to work on the burrito, at which point I felt safe to return to the motel. Never did the notion strike me to stop her. Even if she hadn't come out of the bus station I doubt I would have done anything had the bus pulled in right then to take her away. All this seems less Sarah's right than Sam's—to be spirited off by some young girl in a half-assed caper. And the Sam left with me—thinned to acceptable levels by river dirt and kitchen standards—is exactly what I need and deserve. For these reasons and others I don't want to think about how she will always think me stupid, but maybe that's as it should be. Maybe twenty-three's job is to think almost-forty is stupid. As for almost-forty's job, I haven't a clue. Maybe to realize he can't win, or to just try not to be stupid.

Sam and I take another drive around Hood River, and I recognize more from yesterday afternoon than I do from any time in my youth. I am not looking for a particular house or stream or anything, just driving. The part of my father I am left with appears content with this. After a trip through the McDonald's drive-through we sit in the parking lot near the toll bridge. Windsurfers test the Gorge's morning offering and robust RV families stock up for the hour into Portland or the twenty miles up to The Dalles. I am the kind of full that can only come from too little sleep, too much beer and fatty foods from wrappers. I wipe greasy fingerprints on my jeans and call my mother, grateful to get her voicemail.

"He's gone," I say after the tone, and then head for home.

EXCHANGE RATES

Like so much from those years, that night returns to me first in numbers. Seventy—the minutes since I had turned old enough to vote back in the states. Three—the span from my eighteen years to Shannon's twenty-one. Two thousand three hundred—the elevation we had gained driving up to Whitehorse, Yukon for the Dustball Softball Tournament. Ten to four—the final score by which our team was eliminated that day, with blame for the loss falling on the higher elevation. Two—the number of bars a confident grin and tide of legal-age friends swept me through before Shannon and I struck out on our own. Even now I recall suspecting how these numbers would join all the others that seemed to bear so much weight—GPA's, SAT's, free throw percentages, and so on—to culminate in a grand totaling done some distant place I only knew from television, far from the small northern town which up to that summer was all I had ever known.

I was chasing Shannon around the decks of a sternwheeler now permanently aground where the Yukon River wrapped a sly arm around Whitehorse's lower back. Ninety—the percentage with which I was confident she wanted to be caught. I heard giggles and saw only flashes of the white Western Washington crew sweatshirt she had earned during arduous early mornings on the river. She could have escaped with ease, as evidenced by the honest hustle she had shown today by bringing herself in from third on an infield error.

"Car!"

I rounded a corner to find Shannon on her belly across the refinished planks and literally hit the deck beside her. An RCMP Blazer crawled through a parking lot adjacent to the river boat. A side-mount spotlight lingered on the Alaska plates and equipment bags visible in my mom's 4Runner, the lot's lone occupant. The Blazer itself sighed with knowing relief that Dustball was over and the summer already half-dead. The spotlight made an obligatory sweep of a nearby park's spring-mounted toys and play structure before dimming to head north and await the closing bars' flush of winners and losers, up to their chipped molars with beer and reindeer nachos. July was too early for honest northern lights, but a full moon and something about the earth's tilt promised the sun would not set on all this entirely.

"Just what I need." Shannon jumped to her feet. "Trespassing in a foreign country with a drunk minor."

I shrugged off all but the *minor*. Any government serious about keeping us off the *S.S. Klondike* would do better than easily-jumped chains and padlocks.

"I was ready to sacrifice myself." Only after speaking did I study the ankle-snapping drop to the grass. "Seriously. Like diving on their hood as a distraction."

She was gone again, her comfortable sweats suggesting only muscle and curves with no need for details.

"I'd expect nothing less."

We should have been concerned about being aboard a refurbished landmark most visitors paid six dollars to tour at a normal pace. And I should have been concerned about the

Mounties catching me drunk and underage in two countries, but I was from here and didn't worry. Not from Whitehorse proper, but just a hundred miles south—still *here*. I knew the rivers and where all the pullouts on the highway led and what mountains got the first snow and how much gas I needed leaving Carcross so as to not end up coasting down the pass to town. I knew how far south the Mounties went and how far north the local cops would come to lay in wait. I knew which clouds meant rain and what black ice looked like in headlights and how to get across with only an adrenaline rush. If I am lucky I will someday again feel that much *of* a place, and so sure that things will work out okay.

Shannon had grown up down south in one of Seattle's suburban understudies before heading to Bellingham for school, where I imagined she had tried things with older guys I'd only seen suggested in bathroom graffiti. She had shown interest after two weeks on the cruise ship docks, where I carried the radio and official clipboard of a shore excursion liaison. This was her first summer and I helped her sort through the carnival of confused stares, arthritic hips, shuttle vans and hucksters shouting bargain tours. My calm radio tone and comfort with the grab bag of accents suggested more than my seventeen—now eighteen—years, and though Shannon had backed off a little upon learning my age, I retained hope.

I bore no delusions as to why the summer college crowd allowed me on their softball teams and risked real jail buying me beer, and why I could chase Shannon in such a fashion without her blowing a rape whistle. Anywhere else I would be just another fresh dumbass grad, but up here I was like a stamp on their passport or that lift ticket from Mount Baker they kept on their winter jacket months even after the print faded beyond readability—I was proof of something real, evidence they had been here. In return I found out what bands I should be listening to and what books I should read or at least have conspicuously visible in my dorm room that fall. I got practice being a charming but mellow drinker. Most importantly I learned what kids Outside would be like and I paid attention, so that upon arriving there I would not immediately reveal myself as different from them. The trade seemed a fair exchange for seventeen dark winters of walking to school backwards in the wind and growing up with the same twenty girls who regarded you with the bored familiarity of a brother by the time you were old and brave enough to slip a hand in. They did nothing for fear you would talk—as I would have—and were granted other options sooner. Junior high found them cruising with high school guys, trading up a few years later to the summer college boys. In the seven weeks since graduation I had seen those girls around town, but knew they were gone for good.

Shannon had gone overboard and now stood in the grass near the ramp with its ornamental chain gate. A planted spotlight meant to illuminate the bow silhouetted her hair's more rebellious fringes. She was done running and looked like a rock star.

"Maybe I am," she said when I told her as much, in a drunk bravado that revealed no cracks even under the spotlight. "Tonight, to you."

I slipped over the chains and waited for the witty exchange that too much television had promised would precede real romance. No banter came, but our kiss did, arriving like that fumbling buzzer-beating jumper against Haines my junior year—ugly, yes, but the shot went in and the place exploded. Her lips parted wider than I dared hope and her tongue bragged of White Russians. The seal broken, I started down her jawline only to be trapped when she tightened her neck.

"I stink, Ryan," she said. "I didn't even shower today."

No lie—our team rose at eight a.m. for a consolation-round loss before sweating out a few games on the bleachers and then heading to the Kopper King for chunky burgers and smoky drinks. I didn't care and admitted as much to her thumping jugular. Shannon retook our kiss with an athleticism that soon locked me onto the grass under her thick sweats. The slack hem of her sweatshirt hung like an invitation and I found her ribs first, then her honest underwire—my first outside of that dog-eared section of the *Sears* catalog. For a moment I was sure her entire weight rested on my mouth and left hand.

That beautiful weight lifted, her tongue snapping back like a janitor's key ring. Shannon sat upright, hyperextending my knees, but I didn't flinch.

"This is crazy." She surveyed the old boat and the warm non-committal night above us. "This would have been technically illegal less than two hours ago."

I cited the time change, but the gain or loss of an hour did nothing.

"No. No," she said. "I don't want to mess things up."

"Mess what up? I like you, you like me."

The shadows reclaimed her face, leaving me to hope a smile lay in there.

"God, I'd kill to be eighteen again."

"I wish I was older," I said. "Nineteen. Twenty-six. Maybe even thirty."

Leaning back into me, her hair danced into my collar.

"No, baby, take those numbers back. Don't wish that. Promise me you won't."

I would have promised her that—promised her anything—but her mouth fell back on mine before I had to. Her throat cracked with a groan of at least two-thirds frustration, the remainder I hoped to be surrender. I was back under her sweatshirt and managed to unlatch her bra, leaving it rattling around her shoulders. Hands full of potential grazed my lower back and the perfect mix of muscle and fat danced under my fingers as I made for her drawstring. I attempted to mimic her moans but feared it just sounded as if I were taking a crap. A hand found mine and her lips pulled away, snapping tendrils of spit.

"We can't, Ryan..."

"Don't worry," I said. "I won't get weird or anything. I know it's nothing. Just an extension. Of our friendship, I mean. It's cool."

Her look now suggested I *had* crapped.

"An extension...what?"

"I won't think less of you."

"Gee, thanks." Her hands disappeared in search of the bra as she paused for the most soft and tired of smiles. "I'm sorry, hon, we just can't. I might be pregnant."

I set my full attention to adjusting my jeans, hiding evidence from the person who planted it. She refastened herself like a mother cleaning spit-up off an unplanned child.

"Don't freak." She chuckled. "We didn't do anything, y'know?"

I asked who as she snapped her waistband back in order.

"A little personal, don't you think?"

Unsure of what level of intimacy public dryhumping afforded me, I wordlessly agreed and bit back on a clumsy congratulations.

"Brad," she said without prompting. "Brad the Westours escort."

None of those summer people had last names—Jamie the bus driver, Timmy the cook, Margie in housekeeping, and so on. Now Brad the Westours escort had knocked up Shannon the shore ex. Two summers were ruined with worry and who knew which seasonal surname the kid would inherit.

I nodded when she asked if I knew him. In khaki Nordstrom trousers and Oakley shades, big blond Brad rode herd over select tourist clumps between Seattle and Anchorage every two weeks. The bluehairs adored him and he loved them back, but after their 7:30 bedtime he would always strip to 501's and a snug t-shirt for drinking with fellow collegians. He was personable on the docks and routinely addressed me as "Randy" with such confidence I almost checked my own ID.

"Yeah, I know him."

They met at Western last winter, Shannon explained, where he had been platonically influential in getting her this summer job. Nothing became of the potential she felt down in Bellingham until Brad found himself in town for Pajama Night at the Red Onion last month. Now she was five days late—I could only mirror her reaction to the number and ask if Brad knew.

"God, no." The night's first honest shiver shook her. "I can't drag him into this, at least until I know it isn't just a scare. He has enough stress. He's going to China this fall, you know? Before starting his MBA at the U."

I saw Brad jogging along the Great Wall, a bright yellow Walkman on his hip and headphone cords dancing in his wake, listening to a bootleg of some band I wouldn't hear about until they broke up or sold out, smiling and addressing the locals in their native tongue, if only to call them the Chinese equivalent of "Randy." Shannon heaved securely behind her underwire and the thick sweatshirt absorbed her first few tears. A wipe of her sleeve blended grass stains with mascara around her eyes.

"This fucks up everything," she said. "And right before my senior year. No crew. No parties. Who knows if I'll even graduate. And, Jesus, my parents…"

She fell into me, ratcheting up the sobs. I kissed the crown of her skull and let a few strands of hair cling to my lower lip.

"I'll help," I said. "Whatever you need."

She barely contained the snot that threatened to follow her laugh. "Okay. How?"

I was no longer eighteen—fourteen at the most, and getting younger every second that I stalled. I could sell my Nintendo to a summer hippie or frat-boy baggage handler, or wait tables part-time. I could get another job with an important clipboard, or use my radio to call someone for help.

"It just sounded like what I should say."

Her kiss left the corner of my mouth salty.

"Sweet, sweet Ryan. You don't need this either."

I didn't, but let her settle in and clutch my arm like we were walking into some 1950's prom.

"You are going to make some girl so happy someday. So sweet, so unspoiled."

I shifted in response to the singular *girl*. "Not by choice."

"Don't say that, sweetie. That's what's so great about you. You haven't fucked anything up yet. Promise me you'll try to stay like this. Like this summer. Like right now."

I bit my tongue on that promise and the numbers I wanted to lay out on the grass as proof that I had fucked up. Four—the crucial seconds remaining in our tied 2A tournament opener when I committed that stupid defensive foul, sending their best free-throw shooter to the line. We were left with no time to match his two points and those seconds still hung in my teammates' eyes, even when we were laughing about something totally unrelated. Two—the number of hours I made out with that docile sophomore in the observation lounge of the ferry for mere contact and to kill time during the twenty-hour ride back from a track meet in Sitka, never stifling her suggestions that the tryst might lead to more. Last month I drove past her—mine the street's lone car, her the only pedestrian—and declined to even wave, feeling that would be more cruel than no acknowledgement at all. Sixty-four—the dollar amount held in the money clip I discovered near the dock last August and said nothing about, even when I overheard an ancient couple from the *Noordam* looking for the cash. The clip burned in my pocket and only after all the boats sailed and left me alone on the dock did I separate the bills and send the clip into the bay, where it skidded underwater in alternating glints like a fighting flounder's belly. Things had happened to me.

Shannon soon drifted off in a position only softball, beer and worry could make comfortable. Somewhere beneath her left shoulder my watch lay buried, but I didn't want to wake her and knew doing so would only confirm that some pivotal hour had passed. The night didn't get any colder but I was ready for the sky to dim.

We stayed on the grass until Shannon awoke at four. I rearranged the equipment bags in the 4Runner and we clawed through a clunky sleep before giving up around seven. We left a note for our teammates at the T&M Hotel saying we would see them back home. Shannon requested no radio and bemoaned from beneath her sheltering coat the holy deluge of grief waiting to fall on us for disappearing together. On the more aggressive curves she burped complaints of nausea.

"But I think it's just last night." A brown Yukon morning rolled by, made up of loose dirt and dry trees we didn't have on the other side of the pass. "Still, I guess I should cut back on the drinking. Until I know, right?"

I wanted to say no, that all those studies and warning labels and fetal alcohol syndrome posters were just government propaganda, but came up with only a shrug she took as easily as the undated 222's we had found in mom's glove box. I pulled into the gas station at Carcross, named for the caribou that used to migrate through in droves. The station's food mart was a last chance to purge any Canadian currency before the border. Loonies revealed themselves to me everywhere in the car as Shannon eyed the store.

"What do they have?"

Everything, I said. Though the sixty-five miles to my house challenged the title, this was the only convenience store I knew. Inside waited thick-cut chips with flavors dreamed up by drunken lumberjacks and candy bars so exotic their legality was questionable down south.

"Old Dutch chips. Or Smarties, which are like M&M's," I said. "Or a Crispy Aero is like a Nestlé Crunch. And Coffee Crisp is good."

"What's that one taste like in American?"

Not every candy had a U.S. equivalent, I explained, and well, it tasted like coffee. She agreed to try one with chocolate milk. I made a show of refusing her money and left Shannon stretching against the 4Runner's rear bumper in a July sun that was already lonesome for the minutes of daylight disappearing every day.

Inside, an accent-laden a.m. radio argued with itself about land use issues in places that sounded familiar though I knew they weren't spelled how I thought they were. Both the man behind the register and his lone patron, a boy of about thirteen, appeared local and shared a hint of just enough native blood to get them undue shit in the redneck corners of Whitehorse and hopefully a little government help should they need it. The kid eyed me like I ought to follow the caribou's lead and then went back to fondling the Cracker Jack bags, an attempt to estimate the relative size and value of the enclosed prize. No one needed more lame stick-on tattoos.

"You probably shouldn't be handling them all, Tommy," the register man said. His tone said he didn't own the store, but admitted knowing that if he'd played his cards a little better he could have. "I don't think it's the spirit in which the prize is intended."

Tommy laughed like gravel and slung the candy back in the bin with a lightning wrist.

"Spirit in which the prize is intended," he said. "Nice job— you just lost a fucking sale."

The bell above the door undermined Tommy's theatrical exit and the register man was still smiling when I deposited my snacks before him.

"That's good." He nodded at the door. "Kid don't take any guff. He'll make out okay."

I dumped my Loonies and rainbow of stone-faced dignitaries onto the counter and still received several coins back with a denture plate whistle.

"You've done alright yourself, son."

The man looked beyond me to where Shannon stood outside stretching skyward like all men hope women do every morning whether we're looking or not. Her hip muscles were awake and a soft divot flexed from her lower back.

"Thanks."

"I mean it." His false smile was a whiteout. "Nice lines. Real clean."

I wanted to say no, she actually hadn't showered in two days, had slept in those clothes and stunk up the 4Runner with several rancid farts courtesy of her Kopper King bacon cheeseburger. I said none of this and simply joined the man in staring. I needed to go and had math to prove it. Four—the number of ships that would be awaiting my clipboard and radio work tomorrow. One—the time this afternoon by which I was to return my mom's car or catch holy hell. But already these hard digits were giving way to bigger ones that did not lend themselves to grand totals or winning percentages, maybe just acceptable averages and hopes of breaking even. Ten weeks or so—my time before leaving for college and then four years until graduation, though the national average was drifting towards five. At least two—the number of kids I saw Shannon and Brad ending up with, give or take the one possibly percolating in her belly. Enough—the number of girls I hoped to find ready to keep me company on those nights Brad and Shannon would spend in some cul-de-sac watching television and eating microwave popcorn. Everything beyond that door and bell got more imprecise and uncertain the longer I waited, but I only wanted to stand there and admire the clean lines of the girl I woke up with that morning. I had to walk out there sometime, but not just yet.

PRIORS

Getting eighty-sixed from a place used to take some real doing. Broken chairs or windows, a police car, some spilled blood—and not just a busted lip or split knuckle, but pooled or congealing. Most importantly, a good story was implied, one with details that hardened after each retelling until even the biggest lie rang true. I'm embarrassed to tell anyone how I got banished from that bar back on Burnside, but embarrassed for all the wrong reasons. I wasn't surprised, though. Things there were changing. Slow and steady, like how they say the continents drifted. You think you're safe just staying in one place for thirty odd years and then one morning you wake up to find the rest of the world crowding in through no fault of your own.

I suspect I was booted to lend the place credibility. Lately, everyone there wanted the place to be a dive, and people getting kicked out is a thing that happens at dives. The same way those kids from Lewis & Clark College or the new condos down by the bus station would drag in to drink PBR in their stiff trucker hats and listen to Molly Hatchet on the jukebox before the sun set and they lit off for the safer ground of 23rd or the Pearl District. I didn't have the heart to tell them that you don't *go* to dive bars, but simply end up there without prior intention. Some places aren't like a pre-distressed denim jacket you put on for camera-phone pictures with your friends—they're just the only thing you have to wear when the weather demands. When I was shown the door, there were no cops, no raised voices, no nothing really. And the bartender, for all his black t-shirts and high-end tattoos, could only come up with something flimsy like "I think you'd better leave." Why would I tell anyone that lame jellyfish of a story?

Back in April I picked up a little tax-free construction work outside Home Depot and ended up off Division pouring a driveway with some Mexican guys. Real Mexico—not that Spring Break-Sammy Hagar-Cabo Wabo crap—but they spoke good English with enough accent to make every word they said sound righteous. All three hailed from various villages up in the Sierra Madre, where they had wild pigs that were actually deer and train robbers and whole towns run by *narcos* who would kill you just because you weren't already dead. Over lunch at Plaid Pantry I heard about Chupacabra, which is like their Bigfoot and Dracula and Martians all mashed together. No one had any specifics—he ranged in size from a big dog to a small man and could either jump really far or just outright fly. So far he only terrorized the livestock of *Telemundo* countries, sucking blood from cows and goats and leaving them like old Capri Sun pouches. No human had been hurt or killed yet, but no one wanted to add to the legend. Even under Portland's flat grey overcast, these guys were serious and snuck glances skyward.

Sure, they said, the gringos who went to Cancún or Puerto Vallarta made jokes and liked to tell the stories, but those people were all safe. A fellow needed to go farther in, beyond the Señor Frog's and wet t-shirt contests to places whose names everyone recognized but no one you knew had ever visited.

Their heads shook when I asked about personal sightings, but one guy had heard Chupacabra once, just a chilling whisper overhead while walking the dope trails as a younger man. Despite a grinning shiver he claimed to not be scared.

"Chupacabra won't come for me." He pointed at his two friends. "Or any of us. We believe in him. If he kills everyone who believes, he won't exist anymore."

All this came flooding back to me two Monday nights ago, when Jamie and I hung like bats against the seatbelts of his upside-down Geo Metro, listening to the siren grow louder. The ceiling was full of stray Fritos and straw wrappers and enough change that I was thinking we could get another bottle if we weren't picky. Jamie was crying about three strikes and you're out and losing his license for good and how I was to blame for the whole thing. He had a point since he'd wanted to stay home with *Halo 3* but I made him drive up to the antenna farm because despite living my whole life here I now only recognized this city by the night skyline when viewed from the safe altitude of the West Hills. So our rolling off of Skyline Boulevard technically was my fault, and Jamie losing his license would be bad as he owned the car and drove me wherever I wanted or needed to go. His blubbering annoyed me as much as the idea of riding everywhere on the bus, and I felt confident that the Metro—idling away like a turtle on its back—would be fine if we got a couple guys to help roll her upright. After undoing our belts and crawling out, I looked up for Chupacabra among the antenna lights and my brain just went to work. I had my own priors but remembered something about a seven-year statute of limitations, and though I couldn't recall exact dates my past troubles felt at least that far away. So what if they took my license? I'd never owned anything bigger than a Yamaha 175 and saw no signs of that changing soon. By the time the cruiser's lights painted the trees Jamie's eyes were dry and he promised to drive me anywhere and thank you, thank you, thank you. In short, he believed.

Everyone believed—the officers, my mom when she came to bail me out, even the skinny public defender assigned my case after my arraignment hearing. Only after I explained in confidence the tale I'd spun did he show any hint of disbelief.

"You do realize you're an idiot," he said. "Don't you?"

Turns out my priors, like all those pennies and dimes and fat quarters we had dropped in Jamie's Metro over the years, added up to a respectable sum when the car rolled over. Chances were Jamie wouldn't have to worry about giving me a lift for quite a while. Over that next week I told the real story to whoever would listen but my folks were skeptical and Jamie had grown real fond of the version I dreamed up that night, especially since things weren't as simple as rolling the Metro back over. He told me about bent frames and Blue Book values, but to be honest I lost interest in what he was saying. The whole mess was firming up into a story I didn't really care to hear.

Now I'm watching my court date slip by on a clock with no numbers, just two hands on a metal plate advertising something called Malta Goya. The missing numbers are no big deal, as I'm still unsure of the time zone change and my appointment may already be an hour or two gone. And I think the clock is a few minutes slow to boot. Down the street an unseen band is doing a sound check at an urban amphitheatre, playing a pumping dance number so loud car alarms are going off. Kids gather outside for a peek and a worker two blocks away is catching his siesta in a wheelbarrow. The city buses smoke like they're on fire and the streets around the mall are full of smells that are initially intriguing, though I'm reluctant to breathe too deep for fear the origins aren't what I imagine. You can't make this stuff up.

After the two-day train ride to San Diego, I chose Guadalajara because the city lay deep in the interior of destinations listed

on the Tijuana bus station's wall and I had heard the name
but knew nothing about the place. I've only been here three
days, taking a cheap room near Plaza Del Sol that the savings
account I cleaned out should keep me in for at least another
month. On a long walk I saw all their museums and churches,
which I admit looked the same to me after the first two.
Cars I recognize from up north have different names here,
but the mall has Starbucks and McDonald's and KFC if I get
disoriented. Across from my room a construction crew spent
yesterday knocking down a brick wall. Today they are putting
up one that looks no different. I think I'll make out okay.
English speakers are a little sparse in the bars I've visited, but
if one comes in I guess I'm ready to talk, maybe even share
the lame details of how I got kicked out of that last bar up in
Portland.

To understand you need to know how as a boy in Gresham
my mother would drop me and the neighbor kids off at school
on her way to work, and in return their mom would collect us
all afterwards in her International Harvester Travelall wagon
that wasn't merely painted brown but was in every way brown.
Smell, feel, sound—like a big dry rolling turd with bench seats.
More often than not she was still in her housecoat, which with
the style of the times was probably avocado or canary but in
my mind will also be forever brown. My class always got out
a little earlier than her kids' did, so I would wait with her
in that brown Travelall with the heater and Oregon drizzle
combining to make the windows sweat. We didn't talk because
our pickup time was right when Paul Harvey came on to tell
his stupid stories about children who despite all the hardships
and adversity grew up to be astronauts or presidents or people
I'd heard about on TV. Even after her kids were in the car and
we were headed home I had to listen to this tired old man
whose talking had nothing to do with what I saw rolling by
outside that brown International Harvester.

So there I was at that bar on Burnside last week, enjoying a lunchtime Budweiser and thinking about *nolo contendere* pleas and Chupacabra and Jamie's fucking Geo Metro when the bartender tuned up Paul Harvey on his portable radio behind the taps. There were some younger folks in there and I don't know if the bartender was being funny or ironic or whatever, but he just let the station play. He eyed me funny when I ordered a Red Stripe simply for the stubby little fist of a bottle, and I didn't even crack the cap before sending the beer right into that radio, reducing Paul Harvey into plastic splinters and brown glass shards and cracking the mirror behind. By the time that bartender said "I think you'd better leave," I was already on my way out. And even though I knew I couldn't talk my way out of the DUI I had brought upon myself, I can sure as hell justify what happened to that radio. No one should have to listen to some old man tell you how "that is the rest of the story." What's left of someone's life deserves more than to be reduced to those few pathetic words. They may seem comforting when you're sitting in your housecoat or drinking beer someplace that isn't the place you think it is, but that's just bullshit. No one knows the rest of the story—not some turkey-necked dinosaur on the radio or a judge hiding behind his bench or even your parents shaking their heads over the breakfast table. There is always more. There has to be.

ESCAPE FIRE

'm not from here, but I may as well be. I have called this place home for over twenty-two years, and the city where I grew up Outside wouldn't recognize me on the street. My rare returns to Seattle are like bumping into some third-grade classmate I played little league with but then his family moved away and he went to school for something I know zilch about and we both just stand there toeing the dirt, grasping for anything to say. And since the California transplants and Microsofties blew up the Kingdome a couple years back, I can't think of one damn thing to say to my hometown. I might tell the Space Needle to watch her back, but that's about it.

So I'm from here by default. I knew this the minute I walked ashore off the old ferry dock, a month out of South Seattle Community College with a fresh Associate's degree in diesel and heavy equipment technology. A burgeoning tour company had brought me north to maintain their bus fleet, which the college kids on summer break ran back and forth to Anchorage harder than their beat-up Celicas and B210's back at school. Even then, with my entire twenty-two years slung in a duffel over my shoulder, I felt roots dropping. Nothing taking hold just yet, but slipping out around the soles of my work boots, dragging along soil still moist from a morning rain and ready to sink in should I stand in one place too long. That summer kept me on the highways, up the Taylor and over the Alcan and down the Richardson, driving empty functional coaches to wherever one broke down and working all night with only my tool bag and French-Canadian talk radio stations in the middle of BFN until the bus was running. Every thrown rod or scrapped transmission showed me more country I had never before dreamed existed, and I loved rolling in for a fat breakfast at Jake's Corner or Chistochina driving a bus that would still be dead roadside if not for me, unshowered and working on what even my invincible youth recognized as too little sleep, tracking down a payphone for the collect call telling me where I was headed next. Company policy prohibited hitchhikers but the winter came bitter and lonely and I would have filled all forty-nine seats on that MC8 for a party the whole way home if I'd found enough takers. Mostly I ended up with the occasional out-of-luck drifter, some poor bastard happy for the cramped bathroom and sure that if they just got to Fort St. John or their brother's place up in Palmer everything would work out okay.

The next July found me back in town and fired from that same job three times in twenty-four hours. Some slick kid up from Seattle HQ, wearing pressed pants and a button-up shirt of colors no man who knew better would wear north of Vancouver, took to telling me my job one night at the Red Onion. He'd studied at Western in Bellingham, driven nothing but cake day runs out of Anchorage for a couple summers, and apparently kissed the right asses down in corporate because he was now in charge of the Southeast motorcoach division and knew everything about everything. By ten-thirty I'd had too much Black Label and too much crap from him, so I told him to fuck off. That first time he fired me I didn't take him seriously and popped him in the nose. Nothing too hard, just like you would a friend getting out of line, but enough to drop him off his penny loafers. My second firing—done from behind his bleeding nose on the beer-sticky planks of the bar floor—carried more conviction.

My third and final notice came when I woke up the next afternoon and despite having no reason to stick around, I did. The local railroad, Skagway's cholesterol-laden but long-beating heart, was little more than year away from shutting her doors due to plummeting ore prices and closing mines. In short order a lot of people would find themselves hungry for work and thirsty for a drink. I felt in good company and became just another guy who got by doing whatever job needed doing, stopping only for a beer or a really good practical joke. The next spring I lucked into a deck position on the state ferries, allowing me to see a little more of Southeast and eventually buy my current home, a stout cabin up on the Dyea Road where I could walk out on the front porch and look down over the town, and maybe see where I left my truck the previous night. When the railroad reopened fourteen summers ago as a summer tourist operation, I took a job in the train shops that would keep me on dry land and allow me to get to the bars any night I want and a few I shouldn't. Those roots dangling from my boots when I first showed up are pretty much trees now. Even if I cut them down they would leave stubborn trunks I'd most likely have to poison, then burn, and eventually pull out with a winch.

A lot of people you meet during the summers need you to know they are travelers. They sew patches on backpacks, turn dirty truck canopies into an atlas of bumper stickers, and talk about how in Europe beer is sold at McDonald's and drank warm. When sharing their weed, they inevitably mention the global lengths trekked in pursuit of that special crop. All this may score points at the pub with the passport-and-sandals set, but I figure someone needs to actually be from these places. Someone has to be like those older houses that despite changing hands every few years are still called by the original owner's name. In a place that gets sealed up in plywood and plastic every winter, someone has to be thankful when everyone leaves in September and even more thankful when they return again the next spring.

Others might say my main reason for staying is because I am something of a hero around here. This does let me get away with a lot of shit, but it's usually shit I wouldn't care about getting in trouble for anyway. The hero business was fun for a couple years but eventually got old and stayed that way. Lately the whole matter has become like a creeping fall flu or some rumor that you gave one of the summer girls crabs or anything else you want gone that keeps hanging around. After two decades of being remembered for one damn thing I did, I'm ready to be forgotten for all the little things I do just like everyone else.

This afternoon, a perfect example—I sit in the director's office, knowing full well I am in trouble. With potted plants and a giant computer monitor showing a beach so sunny and faraway the image must be fake, the room's cleanliness make me anxious and I shift in the leather guest chair, making expensive fart noises I can't afford to chuckle at. Professional paintings of trains hang on the wall. I try not to judge, but it strikes me that if a guy washes his hands after taking a leak instead of before and needs paintings to remind him what business he's in, he might not be a railroader anymore. I don't tell the director this, but instead sit there and let this fellow with clean fingernails and a denim company shirt tell me I've been called in for cursing. I should be worried about my job or my reputation, worried about something. But I know things will come out okay and just think how if he keeps talking until 2:55, I can call it a day and stroll straight over to the Red Onion to tell this story. The other day shift guys will probably cut out early and be waiting.

What happened was this: Two days ago one of the narrators, a college kid who rides the coaches with a hands-free microphone and logoed blazer to make sure the passengers don't miss one piece of trackside history, brought her visiting dad into the shops. Being a train buff, the old man wanted to see the nuts and bolts of the operation. Anyone who turns wrenches for a living will tell you the grease that keeps this or any industry's nuts and bolts from squeaking is profanity. The daughter was distracting with her explosion of blonde hair and pneumatic BYU sweater, but for the most part we kept up our usual work and cursing. Apparently her foamer dad didn't want his little girl working around such heathens, and walked straight from the shops down to the director's office in the newly-remodeled depot and gift shop. This rail-nut threatened to drag his fragile flower home to Utah or launch one of those lawsuits that fill the courts down south if the issue wasn't addressed somehow. The end result is me sitting here looking at paintings of trains and a fake computer beach, trying to appear worried when I'm not. The director hopes I understand where he's coming from and I agree and nod at the carpet about fifty times in a row, until even he seems embarrassed and finally walks me to the depot's front doors, patting my back and apologizing for singling me out.

"It's just that the other guys look up to you," he says. "You're sort of a role model. You set the tone, y'know?"

I nod for the fifty-first time and look at my watch. 2:49. Close enough. He walks inside and I make like I am heading around to my work truck but then cut behind the Park Service building and across Broadway to the Red Onion.

Live music rolls out of the bar's front door, mixing with the shuffling gift bags and bus exhaust on the touron-crowded street, loose jazz warning me that the bar will be thick with boat turds. Sure enough, one of the cruise ship bands has shanghaied the bar's gear and is long gone in a masturbatory improvisational odyssey, a necessity after too many vanilla renditions of "Margaritaville" or "Tie A Yellow Ribbon." The audience listens with equal parts cool approval and disinterest. They are primarily mid-tier crewmembers—pursers, shore-ex coordinators or entertainers—all slick-gelled Eurotrash or their U.S. equivalent. They smoke elegantly and sip obscure drinks ordered solely to confuse the bartender so they get the smug enjoyment of explaining how to mix it. If cruise ships were rock concerts, boat turds would be the roadies who tested microphones and got sexual favors from the uglier groupies after promises of backstage access. Few look over thirty-five and none would admit to it, making me wonder where boat turds go when they are too old to sail or entertain. Maybe something humane is in place, like those adoption programs for burned-out greyhounds.

"Randall!"

My name cracks the room like a hammer dropped on a glass table. Even the stony bass player, slipping up and down his frets with no excess movement, casts out a perturbed glance. The Alder brothers wave from the bar. Jason, the younger and more trying, points at an open stool. Cutting through a sea of clean black leather and flammable fragrances, I am disappointed the brothers beat me here. Jason is a hard worker but can't tell a story worth a damn even when he knows all the facts, which he doesn't on this one. No doubt he has mangled the details already. His older brother Sammy is quieter and was still trying to control Jason when they started working with me six years ago. He has since abandoned this mission, save for the occasional shot to Jason's obliques when his younger brother stands to get them in a fight. An infrequent but solid brawler and sibling—more solid than Jason deserves, most agree—Sammy still backs his little brother without question when hands become fists. Even when you know them as well as I do, this blind loyalty hangs around every interaction with the Alders like fine print waiting to bite you in the ass.

Behind the bar is Will, a seasonal vagabond with at least four summers here by my count, who knows your regular drink, knows when you need something stronger, and listens to your stories. Really listens, like looking you in the eye and not wiping the counter or counting tips at the same time. As a bartender he knows that although everyone has a story, eighty percent of drinkers have more or less the same one. More importantly, he knows the value of stories that don't seem worth anything at all.

"It's George Carlin himself," Will says, sliding a perspiring Kokanee my way.

"I guess you want a debrief?"

In unison the Alder brothers say a *fuck yes* they have obviously rehearsed. I give a rundown about the paintings and plants and how we each get a note in our permanent file and that's about all. I hang air quotes around *permanent file*, hoping I'm using them correctly.

"Huh." Sammy looks off across the room. "I didn't know I had a file."

I shrug. "I guess all that information from our permanent files in high school had to go somewhere."

Jason laughs. "You mean the company knows I got caught jerking off in the bathroom in the tenth grade?"

"I think most folks just assume as much," I say.

"Hell, it was under your yearbook picture," Sammy says.

"Whatever," Jason says. "Still beat geometry."

He casts a sloppy smile out over the crowd, hooking a dark beauty who wants so badly to look Mediterranean she must be from Nebraska or Wyoming. The scowl she sends back says if Jason were stuck to her knee-high black boot, she wouldn't just wipe him off but rather throw the boot away and go barefoot.

"I hate boat turds," he says.

"It's only today," Will says. "*The Legend Of The Seas* is pulling out late tonight."

We talk about work and the blonde in the BYU sweater and how none of us will be able to make the Dustball tournament in Whitehorse this weekend, though Sammy—his punching arm also good for no-bounce throws from centerfield—is the only one who will be missed. My first pain hits just as a silver tourist couple makes room where there isn't any beside me at the bar. The man glows red like a constipated keg and wears an "Alaska Bush Pilot" hat so new the bill could slice bread. I smile hello while my gut twists like a groin kick has crawled up my spine.

He correctly pegs us as residents, and starts a lazy tirade about how he has yet to find a campground to park his twenty-four foot Itasca for the night that is not overcrowded and how expensive everything is compared to back home. A goddamn racket, he says. I can only assume he lives somewhere no one will ever want to visit. His wife is dolled up in a white jumpsuit and was probably something else back during that OPEC crisis, but her price per barrel is definitely down. Jason gladly assumes the conversational lead, allowing me to take a few hidden stabilizing breaths and grind my teeth so hard I fully expect to taste enamel splinters or the ancient mercury filling from my back molar.

After a few minutes I feel the welcome waning of the pain, like an out-of-tune marching band trudging steadily away down the street. I disguise my honest grimace as a response to the man's tale of paying thirty-five dollars Canadian for a spot and hookup at the only RV park in Dawson Creek with a vacancy and then getting hit for another five to dump and the

damn GST on top of that. We unanimously agree everything
should be included in a single fee.

Finally confident I can walk, I play the gentleman and offer
the wife my bar stool. In the bathroom I wait for a stall, not
wanting to alarm any wandering eye at a neighboring urinal.
At first peeing blood freaked me out, but it really isn't a big
deal now. I can tough out the aches and pains when sitting
down, and I've worked hard to put together a life that lets me
sit down whenever I want. I can even handle the thought of a
little crystalline burr tearing and clawing down my plumbing
with lazy plans of escape. Staring down at the shiny bowl tinted
red in a freshly-repainted restroom with classic rock dropping
down from a satellite into the speakers, what really gets me is
I just feel old.

At forty-four, I realize I am getting on, but never before
have I felt old. Having these floating retirement homes drift in
every summer helps. Compared to the average tourist they send
ashore, who requires a shuttle for the quarter-mile between the
dock and the downtown gift shops, I still look like Charles
Atlas. But another reason I've hung around so long is that this
place allows me to continue feeling young, a right I should have
long ago surrendered. Skagway is always new to someone, be
it the comfortable slacks-and-Camcorder crowd in for a day or
the seasonal gypsies. Someone is always discovering and falling
in love with this town, and I am part of it all and perpetually
fresh and new somehow, just like when I first showed up here.
Back then I felt like the latest and greatest model and so did
everyone I knew. We drank like we had just invented beer and
whiskey and laughed like no one outside the city limits was in
on our joke. There were older people around here, but they
just stayed older or eventually died, leaving us to always feel
younger than them. The kids from when I arrived went from
bikes to cars to colleges to buying me drinks at the bar, but
when I look at them I still see kids. Even the little girl whose

life I saved to start all this hero bullshit. She used to giggle when I bounced her on my knee, and now she's twenty-two and bouncing in a whole different way. To me, she'll always be that little creature with thin brown hair, clinging to my shoulder in Strawberry Shortcake pajamas while we stood under a light snow watching the fire.

I guess I somehow figured things would just stay that way, even after some of us sprouted grey hair or man-boobs and a few even had children on purpose. And while people still recognize us and know who we are, somewhere along the way all our streets got paved and driving drunk stopped being funny. The friendly little *Love Boats* the town originally opened her doors to grew into fortresses that now loom over Broadway like a raised-brow boss warning us to shape up and get to work, and God knows we need the job. Each morning thousands scramble ashore ready for everything promised by the website or brochure they saw in Illinois, demanding proof and settling for nothing less. Shops pushing diamonds and furs have popped out of empty buildings, staffed by people who aren't interested in learning my name, who will be peddling the same crap to the same boats in St. Thomas or San Juan in six months. We have been discovered and lost at the same time, and the whole phenomenon went down in the way I imagine it feels to cross the international dateline on a ship. Everything you see passing outside looks no different than all the water you've drifted through before, but then you look up and it's not the day you think it is. Then you are pissing blood and some Canadian doctor says if things don't pass in two months he'll break up the stone with a laser and a director tells you to watch your language because you're a role model. Feeling young, or at least not feeling old, is a little more work every time my alarm clock goes off.

Back at the bar the tourist couple is gone and my stool is occupied by a rear end you could bounce quarters off. Even the aloof male boat turds shift their nonchalant appreciation from the jazz and search their pockets for change, maybe something shiny and foreign to impress this local girl. I will be standing a while.

Here is Janey, the little thing I saved. Her hair looks like she spent all afternoon rolling in tall grass and flowers, and despite an overcast June her tan from a University of Arizona winter hangs on her in a manner that this bar's male population dreams of. Her grin is all that allows me to fit her back into those pajamas.

"Corrupting Mormon girls now?" she says.

I reach around her for my beer. Keep the fluids up—doctor's orders. "Well, it wouldn't be right to discriminate by religion."

She squeezes my hairy forearm and hijacks the Kokanee before I can set the bottle down.

"I didn't think a railroad could run without profanity," she says.

"It can't," Sammy says. "It's in our Teamster contract."

"Well, times change," Jason says, buzzing good and reeling in his twenty-six years. "I mean, who ever thought we'd be buying alcohol for this little girl?"

"Legally, you mean." Janey slides me a conspirator's glance—you save someone's life, a bond is formed that goes beyond federal or state laws. Or at least that was going to be my defense. Janey derides all of us for planning to miss Dustball, a regional tournament up in Whitehorse that is about softball in the same way strip clubs are about actual dancing. The handful of serious teams soon eliminate the ones we play on, leaving us to drag our hung-over selves out of shared hotel rooms to play consolation games at vindictive hours. Throw in a one-hour time change, an elevation gain of two thousand feet and stronger beer and my head begins aching on memories alone.

"My folks are having a barbeque next Thursday," Janey says to me. "They wanted me to make sure you knew. All the usual suspects, same script. You in?"

"I am," Jason says. His words skip off across the bar like a flat stone. Before I can answer, Will slides a fresh Kokanee between Janey and I.

"Don't forget," he says. "Rod and Gun Club meeting that night."

I roll my palms in defeat. "Sorry, Janey. I'm hosting at my place."

She huffs, expanding her Abercrombie and Fitch t-shirt in an advertiser's dream. "You guys are like Cub Scouts with beards and booze."

Will shakes his head while wiping the bar. "Actually, with the knots and uniforms, Cub Scouts are surprisingly militaristic."

Janey stands and circles my wrist like the weakest of afterthoughts.

"Please try to make it anyway. Karen will be there. She says she had a great time the other night."

Young chatty Karen—during our drunken romp after the annual Soapy Smith's wake last week, I'd kissed her hard on the mouth through our entire one-hour session. What I imagine she took as wanton ardor was simply a quest on my part for beautiful wordless silence.

"Yeah, she's alright," I say. "A bit of a talker..."

"I'll tell her you'll be there."

"I will try my best," I say. "But you know what that's worth."

She pulls a parting kiss from my Kokanee.

"Everyone does."

Like a kicked rubber ball, Janey is out the door onto the playground of the street. Soon she is lost in a sea of relaxed-fit jeans, age spots and blocky plastic sunglasses.

Jason eyes me. "Which one is Karen?"

I shake my head, feigning modesty. Any description I came up with would be half conjecture and sadly inaccurate.

"One of Janey's friends."

"We should all have a guardian angel like that," Sammy says.

"Guardian pimp, y'mean," Jason says. "You got lucky with that one, brother."

"Not lucky," Sammy says. "He did the right thing when it had to be done."

My bar stool is suddenly uncomfortable, and I stand to finish my beer.

"Anyone here woulda done the same." I glance at Jason. "Well, maybe not you."

He rewards me with a rat's grin and his middle finger. I rap my empty on the bar.

"Well, gents, I have to get the work rig back up to the shops for swing shift," I say. "I'll see you tomorrow. Will, next Thursday."

Will holds up the twenty I left with a nod of thanks.

"Rod and Gun," he says.

"Rod and Gun, pal."

When Janey was in elementary school she brought me her drawings. Crayon sketches of her neighbor's cat, or a watercolor boat and sunset, all horrible—the poor girl simply had no eye for art. Later she came around with homemade cookies or free tickets for the rifle or snowmobile her class was raffling off at the high school. A few years ago she began bringing me coeds. Mainly summer girls she meets working at the hotel, sometimes a fellow Arizona Wildcat up visiting for a couple weeks. Janey tells them how funny and charming I am, and probably all the lifesaving crap when I'm not within earshot. She drops these girls on my porch with no definite instructions and eventually leaves us alone. I assume I am to sleep with them—that's what I did before Janey became my booking agent—so I do.

Anyone who has taken basic college psychology—maybe Janey's gabby friend Karen has, I can't recall—could read something into the whole arrangement, but I choose not to dwell on it much. I once came up with what I thought was a witty remark about looking a giftwhore in the mouth, but even the Alder brothers judged it in bad taste. All I know is the help is appreciated. My patience and wit have definitely waned in recent years, and despite her prattling on about topics I don't think even she was interested in, my evening with young Karen still beat Janey's artwork and her best platter of from-the-box brownies.

I had been working the ferries less than a year when I saved Janey's life. I went out a week at a time and did everything from bowlines to painting trim. I enjoyed seeing all the other villages along the shores of Southeast and even more loved the feeling of walking back up the dock to what was starting to feel like my home. Skagway was still hemorrhaging residents from the railroad closing, and a smart man would've saved up six months worth of paychecks and bought the city outright. At the time I settled for a rented singlewide on a bare lot at the north end, across from the dormant train shops and walking distance from downtown with even the most wicked norther blowing.

Janey's folks lived only four blocks south but we ran in different circles, though at the time there were maybe two circles in town. Janey's father Stuart had moved them up from Oregon six months earlier to manage the bank and wore Skagway's only tie. His wife Vicki led the local ladies in aerobics three nights a week at the school's multi-purpose room and looked better after class than anyone else did before. She smiled to everyone at the market and post office and eventually relaxed enough to wear baggy sweats under her expensive winter jacket, but to me she felt distant as those ladies on *Dallas*.

Their house caught fire on a Friday in November, twenty years ago this fall. Stuart and Vicki were across the street with a church group organizing some fundraiser for another railroad family down on their luck, and Janey slept at home under the watch of a moody sixteen-year-old named Sondra. I had never seen this girl smile or talk to anyone, which left her plenty of time for babysitting and moping. In the previous year her body had popped out like a life raft in strategic places, though she hid recent developments under loose dark clothes and you couldn't detect anything unless you looked real hard. The high school boys who did notice still kept their distance, like they would around a bully with new toys. If there had been a college nearby she would have dated the older guys, hanging around the art department or sulking over fancy coffee at poetry readings. Instead Sondra remained alone and appeared to be just biding time, waiting for graduation or something else to save her.

The fire chief later figured the ignition source to be some cleaning supplies placed too near the furnace, between Janey's room and the living room where Sondra sat writing in her journal. Cut off and not willing to risk the flames for three dollars an hour, Sondra dialed 911 and ran across the street to fetch Stuart and Vicki. The church group arrived to find the windows glowing orange and flames licking out around the structure's midsection. They also found me standing in the driveway, holding two-year-old Janey in those Strawberry Shortcake pajamas. My shoulder bore a few minor cuts from the broken window, but I'd been downtown since three p.m. and didn't feel much pain. Vicki hugged me too many times to count while Stuart walked in nervous circles looking at the house until the fire truck arrived. He finally offered some awkward mix of a handshake, formal introduction and a hug. Sondra just eyed me from the sidewalk, arms crossed beneath a chest that grew by the minute.

The volunteer fire department put out the blaze with the help of a thick night snow, and the rest of the populace showed up to watch. I explained to the chief how I had heard crying while walking home and saw flames and the Tot Finder sticker on her window. When the blaze was out, several volunteers dragged me back down to Moe's Bar for a congratulatory round. Stuart went to the fire hall to make phone calls, so

Vicki and Janey came along with us. We all drank rum and Cokes while Vicki and I wore fireman helmets and Janey slept atop a bed of coats on the pool table.

That's the whole deal and I've been a goddamn hero ever since. Vicki and Stuart still have me over for holiday dinners and any other time I want. When the railroad reopened and I was ready for a job on dry land, the hiring man had a kid in Janey's class so I was a shoe-in for a nice warm spot in the train shops. Now when I get a little too drunk and say the wrong thing or drop my truck in the ditch on my way home, people just shrug and say, "That's Randall, he's a good guy at heart." Depending on who I chose as a victim, I could probably get away with murder or at least second-degree manslaughter.

Only the dark and brooding Sondra might take the stand against me. I always wondered if she collected her full pay for that night's work. I never did ask, but instead watched from a safe distance as she grew into a stunning, angry girl who took off to art school down south the second she graduated. I wanted to corner her sometime and just talk—talk in the grownup way I knew she was capable of even back on that night when she was only sixteen and watching snow fall on that burning house. I wanted to know what she remembered and how the fire looked through those rich brown eyes. But we never talked and maybe everything she knew or wanted to say came across in her sharp glance, the same one she started giving me that night in the driveway and gave me right up until she got on an afternoon ferry eighteen Junes ago and never looked back.

At first Will and his friend Colson were reluctant to let me into their Transmontane Rod and Gun Club. They appropriated the name from a group of WWII soldiers who after the war returned to their Army training grounds in the Colorado

Rockies and were instrumental in settling the original ski
towns. The real places, Colson insisted, based on love of place
and a concept I still don't totally get called *Idraet*, not today's
glossy amusement parks full of trust-fund kids and movie
stars. The club's title was supposed to be ironic, Colson said,
like the original group who had nothing to do with rods or
guns but rather a way of life. This conflicted with my actually
owning a closet full of rifles and shotguns and fishing poles
that, placed end to end, would circle my cabin. Colson could
talk all he wanted about irony and mission statements and his
Idraet, but I knew what this club was really about. Drinking
and screwing off was foremost, but running a close second was
a search for something now long gone. Maybe it was a place or
time or thing, maybe we wouldn't know what that something
was until we found it, but they wanted to find that something
and save it or bring it back to life. I knew whatever they sought
lay back in the past, and with more than twelve years on both
Colson and Will, I felt a little closer to that place. I became the
third member and sergeant at arms. Most meetings are held at
my cabin, moved here from the downtown bars when Colson
suspected neighboring drinkers of joining the club's ranks by
default of just sitting at an open table.

Colson lays claim to both president and treasurer titles, as he
started the club and is loaded with cash. If not stinking rich his
family at least emits a very strong odor, and he is dependently
wealthy in a way that lets him get chunky and not care and makes
a person feel a little safer because he considers you a friend, like
he'll buy you a new life if he breaks the one you're currently
using. At thirty-two he has worked most of the summer jobs out
of boredom and lives off his folks, New England flower children
who sold out early on and made jillions off mass-produced
health drinks. He readily admits they simply pay him to keep
his distance, a job he does gladly and with grace.

Even if Colson *is* the financial brawn of the club, I can't call

Will the brains. Rather he is a vague policy advisor who just smiles and nods when he concurs with the course being plotted, and gazes out the window when he disagrees or loses interest. He's merely a good guy who has taken seasonal wandering to an art form, and if anything he is the club's spirit. In an organization that lags a decade or two behind what we are chasing, this role is more important than it sounds.

The remainder of the club is rounded out by summer folk—tour drivers, wait staff, bartenders, and whoever wants to spend every other Thursday listening to Colson drone on about how the big tour companies are killing little towns like ours. Attendance ebbs and flows with the weather and co-ed softball schedule, and this week the sun shines and a game lies visible far down below my porch. Only two additional members have shown up.

"This is good." Colson paces the room around an archaic overhead projector bought last year at a high school auction. "I wanted a tight group, a core."

"Did anyone bring snacks?" This from Jimmy, a Connecticut turbo hippie who guides raft trips down the Taiya River out in the Dyea valley, a waterway that runs wild as a spayed housecat. "All I've had today are like seven Lunchables."

His friend and fellow rafter George agrees, talking about how they were able to smoke a bowl between every run today while the *touristas* took pictures and tightened life vests around their buffet-bloated torsos. By day's end they were starving, but George assures us that his raft cruised down the river like some hybrid of a Cadillac and an oil tanker.

I send them searching for the bag of thick-cut Canadian chips that seems to be under the sink whenever I open the cupboard, even after I could swear I finished them off. Colson draws the shades and shuts out my lone living room lamp, which combines with the oak cabin's natural darkness to drop us into a night we won't see outdoors until September. He fires up the projector, filling the adjacent screen with a black and white image of a Navy landing craft, her jaw dropped and belching GI's out onto some long-ago doomed beach.

"I give you the club's next project," he says.

"Liberating Europe?" I say.

Will whistles. "We're definitely going to need the rest of the guys."

"Very clever," Colson says. "Anyway, this is a LCT Mark VI landing craft, one hundred plus feet long and military born and bred. There's one down in Prince Rupert right now for sale. The first few decades of her life are classified, but she's spent the last ten years shuttling between the logging camps in B.C. She's already been modified with a small galley and bunks. Gentlemen, this boat is perfect for *Three Sheets to the Wind*."

Colson replaces the slide with a sketch of his own doing, a design everyone in the room has seen before only on cocktail napkins. *Three Sheets* is to be a floating brewery, sailing the Inside Passage selling liquor brewed on board to fishing and charter boats and anyone who wants to tie up. It has been Colson's dream for the five years I've known him, and something everyone in the Transmontane Rod and Gun Club has offered false encouragement for under the assumption that common sense and Coast Guard regulations would intervene before the idea gained any real traction. Now Colson has located a craft missing only brewing pots and a crew. When he opens the shades, excuses fly in the light like awakened moths. Jimmy has grad school, George plans on backpacking through Thailand all winter, and Will is off to an undetermined Caribbean island.

"Randall?" Colson says. "I need a man who can handle a torch and knows diesel engines. If I finalize the sale by October we can be in Prince Rupert by November, maybe sailing by the first of the year."

I think of last New Year's Day—forty knots blowing out of the north, drifting snow and whipping the bay into white caps. I stayed huddled on my couch, feeding my wood stove and pulling dirty movies and football down from space with my satellite dish. January, hurry up and get here.

"Sorry, brother, I've got plans."

"Dammit, Randall," he says. "I was especially hoping for you."

A series of small tremors dance through Colson's soft bulk, the beginning of the breakdown that comes like clockwork at every meeting. Like his sloppy haircut and t-shirts for long-gone rock bands, these tantrums serve as a reminder that despite all his moralistic grandstanding and contempt for big Outside money, Colson is by nature a spoiled baby. These episodes are really less tantrum than mild seizure, and we long ago recognized the safest course of action was to just let him go and prevent him from biting off his tongue. I explain calmly that I've already done my time on the Southeast waters and winter is my time to recuperate. Colson asks recuperate from what exactly and I hem and haw. He knows the operation shuts down for four months every winter and most railroaders without families get out for a month or two. The younger ones head to obscure points in Southeast Asia or Europe or some other supposedly undiscovered yet crowded paradise, while the older guys favor the safe standbys of Hawaii and Mexico. I still haven't decided if I am young or old, so I just stay in my cabin.

The ancient overhead projector rescues me. The machine emits a buzzing groan from its guts, coughs a puff of smoke out a side grate, and the upper third of the screen drops dark. Betrayed on all fronts, Colson adjourns the meeting and sets to work extracting a bulb I would wager went out of production in 1973. His announcement does nothing to change my living room's landscape. Will flips through my records, picking out that John Prine LP with the picture of him kicked back and all cocky in some hot little convertible. Will knows I have Prine's greatest hits on CD, but we both like the hisses and pops that wrap around the vinyl album's songs of sweet revenge and blue umbrellas like there was a fire crackling in the studio during the recording session. I tell Will about an old flame who said Prine had the best "Ah, baby," of any singer she knew, how his delivery just gave her shivers down to her toenails and back up to her hips. I had put scratches on my records trying to listen to his inflection and practice that gravel-in-syrup tone. When Will asks I cannot remember the flame's full name or where in the world she ended up, but I can still see her face, and can still nail that "Ah, baby."

Riverraft Jimmy and George are pretty far into my good hooch and getting loud, so I give them my old Rossi pump .22 with a pocketful of rounds and send them down the trail I've carved out to the river. Four summers ago I fashioned a little shooting range where the trees and evening wind muffle the shots, and the trail is tame enough to be climbed drunk and with whatever mild injury a .22 Long might inflict.

Colson gives up with the projector and turns the music up just enough. He and Will look around my cabin as they always do, like a museum or antique shop. I have some packrat blood and the bad habit of setting a item down for a minute and picking it up ten years later, leaving the place somewhere between a scrapbook and a junkyard. I often get a notion to clear the whole cabin's interior into a burn barrel, like an Indian tribe I read about once in high school used to do, and start over from scratch. But then Will or Colson will pull some postcard out of the stack and ask who sent it or what the story is on some old padlock I kept for a forgotten reason on the kitchen counter. I tell them and they just listen, looking right at me and rolling whatever they asked about in their hands, like what they are holding might be worth something. Those times make me feel like all the screwing off I've done might bear a little weight. I get a lot of hints to the contrary, so it does me good to have Will and Colson around.

Tonight they have found a stack of photos from the summer of 1980, my first season here. I bring three fresh beers and we work through the pictures, which I'd found in an ammo case last spring and set out with the intent of cataloging or tossing in the trash. Most are from the 4th of July. The floats all bear the dirt of the then-unpaved downtown streets, and Will and Colson laugh as I point out which shaggy longhairs in the photos they only know as parents, city councilmen or business owners. Kids now grown with kids of their own pedal in the bike brigade, and the local boy who six years ago ran off the highway near Carcross and killed himself along with the oldest Walters girl throws cheap hard candy from the fire truck in a *Maui 78* t-shirt. There are shots of pie-eating contests and the egg toss, but the biggest attraction that year was a Fire Department fundraiser where two bucks got you one swing with a sledgehammer at a defeated Plymouth Valiant donated by the Somdahl family. Most guys took the easy shots at the windows and mirrors or just embarrassed themselves, underestimating how hard a sledgehammer is to use. I was still an unknown and wanted to prove something and talked the fire chief into six swings for ten bucks. I went a little crazy on the Plymouth's back end, bending the trunk in like a loveseat and jumping up to drop my last hit onto the roof. Bystanders clapped and hooted, but many eyed me funny or shuffled their children off for the sack race.

Will laughs at a shot of me standing on that caved-in trunk, still holding the sledgehammer. I can't recall who snapped the picture, but I am staring right at them, and I do look like something else. I'm twenty-five pounds lighter with long sweaty-ass hair down in my eyes, which lie dark behind cheekbones that push out like glass. I hold the sledge like a baby or a bomb and my mouth bears what at the time felt like a grin. When Will and Colson continue through the stack, I slip out the sledgehammer photo and, when I think they aren't looking, slip it into the breast pocket of my work shirt. I like that picture. I like that guy. He is nobody's hero.

I leave my cabin about eight o'clock like a campfire I trust to burn itself out. Will and Colson know which doors I lock and which I don't and where I keep the first aid kit. Walking through the gate at Stuart and Vicki's party I know I screwed up. Everyone sports clean clothes and some are dressed as if attending a warm-weather funeral or graduation. The plates are firm and made of colorful plastic instead of paper. Janey's college-aged friends are actually playing croquet. This is not the kind of party you arrive at already drunk, maybe not even the kind you leave from drunk.

"Randall. Glad you made it."

Stuart is on me from nowhere, holding a platter of still-sizzling beef patties and bratwurst. He wears a prep shirt of a green that doesn't occur in nature, tan shorts with a crease and white socks that even I recognize as hoisted too high. Two decades in this town and he still moves around like he expects his lunch money to be stolen.

"Thanks, Stuart. Nice spread."

I pluck a sausage from the plate and pop its greasy head into my cheek. Stuart shifts like he needs to piss.

"We have plenty of condiments. Buns, plates, napkins. If you want."

I sheepishly step over to the table, slipping my stupid half-dog into a full bun. This satisfies something in my host.

"So," he says. "Your summer going well?"

I assure him it is, choking down a mouthful of plain bun. We talk about how dry July has been and how the valley needs rain. Stuart speaks of his pending business trip to Seattle later this summer and we agree how that city has changed. He outlines his and Vicki's complete travel itinerary but loses me among the big buildings near Pike Place Market.

Only after Janey and Vicki join us does Stuart feel safe to distribute the cooling meat. Both women recognize my drunkenness and flank me for stabilization.

"I'm glad you're here," Vicki says. "This thing might need a little mouth to mouth."

"It's not that bad, mom," Janey says. "It's just mellow. And Karen is here, Randall. I think she's inside making margaritas, but I'll go find her."

Great—perhaps I'll get lucky and develop a speedy bout of food poisoning from Stuart's version of medium well. Janey leaps into the social current and is swept into a youthful eddy, leaving me with Vicki. We ask about each other's summers, though the fact that she is throwing a party with a croquet set and I am in attendance is answer enough for both of us. Vicki no longer looks like the ladies on *Dallas,* or maybe she just looks like those women do now. She often has a few drinks too many and confides various things to me—tonight she suspects Janey is taking the pill and Stuart looks at pornography on his home computer under the guise of work. Why she shares such matters I haven't a clue. Maybe she feels she owes me these personal details for saving her little girl. Or maybe she assumes I am too drunk to remember or care, allowing her to get this business off her chest to a real person without actual feedback, like yelling all your inner fears and dreams and regrets into a stand of trees or a deep chasm, where at most you might get an echo.

In truth I feel for Vicki, the same way I felt for that red 1968 Mustang I had barged up years ago when my deckhand pay started adding up and the Klondike Highway was finally paved enough so that you could go over forty without tearing up your suspension. That Mustang lived a little when I owned her—we did the Dyea road in reverse in less than fifty minutes and spent a night stuck up to the rims in the mud of the Flats until Mark Evers came by to pull us out—but she'd been built for highways, not washboard dirt. I finally sold the Mustang to a kid from Tagish who planned to drive her to Toronto and become a rock star, maybe the next Randy Bachman. I have no idea how far they got, but every once in a while when I'm up in Whitehorse, I scan the posters in the record stores for his face.

"Hey, stranger." Young Karen is on us like a swarm of chatty bees. I turn to Vicki, but like that Mustang she is gone with a knowing speed.

"Janey said you'd be here," Karen says.

"And here I am," I say. "I need a beer, you?"

I dash to the cooler, downing my first bottle on the return trip and then doubling back for another. Walking back, I take Karen in for perhaps the first time ever and must admit that there's nothing truly wrong with her. In her early twenties and with all the parts in the right place, she is smart enough to breeze through a state school and bears many of the common traits I notice in her generation. Her smile is an ironic facsimile of honesty learned from sitcoms and MTV hosts, looking like she knows better but wants something to regret down the road. She also possesses some innate sense as to when something bears weight or value even where I suspect she doesn't see any real worth—like the Steve Miller Band's *Greatest Hits 1974-78* album or Bruce Lee movies or maybe even me. For just this reason I am pretty sure she would happily join me at my cabin tonight and I remind myself I should want that, noticing how her baggy painter pants hide the soft curves lurking underneath and her sweater is doing someone named Hollister proud. Still, if a wild croquet shot heads my way I can't promise to duck.

She takes her beer. "So what's the deal?"

With, I ask.

"Us, dude."

I scan the yard. Is all this really going to go down right here, alongside people neatly eating barbeque with Stuart-supplied Wetnaps and innocent children scurrying around?

"I mean, I haven't heard from you since that night at your place." She doesn't even have the decency to look awkwardly at the ground, but instead eyes me like I've been caught lifting a twenty from her purse.

"I just thought it was a thing," I say. "Y'know, a one-night stand."

Karen emits a horselaugh, catching the attention of a strong young buck playing croquet. She sends him a calming nod.

"First, man, no one has one-night stands anymore, or at least calls them that. Maybe divorced parents in their fifties."

"Huh," I say. "What's it called now?"

"Hooking up. Or friends with benefits. Or fuck buddies."

"That makes sense."

Karen crosses her arms. "So is that what we're looking at for the rest of the summer?"

Already this lingo rubs me like new work boots. "Which do you mean? Fuck buddies or hooking up?"

"Any of them."

A celebration erupts across the yard. The young buck has scored one hell of a shot and insists Karen come join them. She gives him a wave loaded with promise before looking back my way.

"Well," I say. "I guess none of the above."

Finally Karen looks just plain pissed off, something I can work with.

"That's pretty weak, dude."

Guilty as charged, I can only agree. She huffs and cocks her hip like a shotgun she keeps loaded.

"Y'know, Randall, you might be some hot shit up here in your own little solar system, but I'm beginning to think you're nothing but hype." She draws deep from her beer and looks me up and down, like a shirt purchased on impulse finally out from under the flattering dressing room lights. "I mean, you could shower more often, and you're nothing special down below."

"I've heard."

Karen spins sharp enough to divot Stuart's manicured lawn. Off to claim her mallet, she calls back over her shoulder without even a glance.

"You're also a selfish lover."

This is new, and catches a few stray ears who busy themselves adjusting the load on the fine plastic plates. The young buck takes her into the game with a lingering hug that strays below the waistline and stays there. The shit kids can get away with these days. The intensity of Karen's practice swings suggests now is a good time for an exit.

On my way out I grab a plate for one pass by the food table. There's chicken, chips, warming potato salad and various expensive regional lagers that only the seasonal folks are drinking. I jam a few in my jacket pockets and head to the gate, trailing food but not looking back. I offer a few waves of greeting and thanks and my hand is on the gate when I hear my name. I turn to see Janey running my way, holding a chicken leg garnished with this morning's lawn clippings.

"You dropped this."

On closer inspection, moist soil clings to the bone.

"Thanks, but I'm set."

Janey sends the chicken leg off with a perfect set shot courtesy of four years as a varsity basketball starter. The leg rattles into a garbage can fifteen feet away, several dogs growling in lost hopes of a rebound.

"You can't stay?"

"Y'know, obligations."

"I talked to Karen."

"Already?" Across the lawn Karen laughs with her fellow players. "Do you guys communicate in shorthand?"

Janey smiles. "Yeah, like texting."

"Like what?"

"Never mind." She pulls a sweating bottle from my jacket. "Besides, your relationships don't lend themselves to long discussions." She eyes the plate and my choices. "Anyway, she thinks I'm trying to change your mind, so let's at least sit down and act like it."

We take an empty table near the gate, offering a view of the party's guts. Stuart prowls the perimeter like a pro-wrestling referee overseeing a staged battle royal already slipping from his control. Karen sneaks glances between shots. Vicki laughs too hard at some comment by our lone insurance broker, who in my entire time here I've never heard say anything remotely funny.

"So, are you trying?" I say.

"No, but I said I would. That's what friends are for."

I start into my potato salad. "So I guess we just sit here and bullshit, then we hug goodbye and you tell her I'm still grieving from Paula or Tera last summer and I'm not ready to be hurt again."

The potato salad needs more dill. I wonder which dishes Janey made and when I can politely stop eating.

"What's her deal, anyway? That side of beef seems pretty fond of her."

Janey nods in agreement at the young Adonis.

"Sure, Chad's great. He's fun and can do pushups all day. But there are a million like him out there. When we decide we want one we can just pick the model we like. But you're different, like an old car…"

She notices my look and I feel safe to put down my fork.

"A classic car," she says. "No one is making them anymore. Besides, you're like hiking the Chilkoot or doing the Fourth of July egg toss. A rite of passage."

The sun is dropping behind Face Mountain and getting ready to hit this party just right.

"No wonder I have you doing my recruiting."

Janey follows her smile with a grimace. "Yeah, but we're starting to dry up the student base on the West coast. I'll have to go to grad school back east for some fresh blood."

"I hear Michigan is nice." We laugh even as my innards tighten in a familiar way. I let my face stiffen as if in deep thought. "Janey, have you ever heard the term one-night stand?"

"I think mom accused dad of having one when I was eight or nine," she says. "Wasn't it an eighties thing, like swinging?"

"Yeah, I guess so." The damn gremlin is rolling down my piping for sure now, like a softball with nails driven through at all angles. I want to double over and fall into Stuart's thick green grass, letting the cool moisture soak into my clothes. I want to do those breathing exercises doctors make pregnant ladies learn, to yell or scream or punch something even if it hits me back twice as hard. Instead I just grip my beer, waiting for the bottle to shatter and drive shards into my sweaty palm.

"I ask them, you know," Janey says.

"Come again?"

"Karen, Paula, Tera—I ask all of them," she says. "What it's like, what you're like. Most tell me to begin with, but if they don't I ask."

Janey crosses her arms and leans back. She's a little drunk but not *that* drunk. We all deserve to be this unafraid, and long past the age of twenty-two.

"Why?"

"To know what all the buzz is about."

My gut wrings itself like a burlap sack. I lean forward to tighten up our conversation and wrap myself around the pain.

"I could argue that you're the one behind all the buzz."

Janey shakes her head. "You had this racket going long before I came along." She looks over to Karen, who no longer glances our way. "I'm just a salesman. A salesman who's never used the product."

"Maybe that's why you're so good at selling it."

I can only smile—this is literally all I can do. I grit my teeth so hard against my twisted burning insides I expect a crown to pop through my cheek. The sweet beautiful smile that reflects back on my own only knows such pain from movies and Tylenol commercials.

"So I ask," she says. "And I think I know now. I know how you're going to touch my chin and gently thumb my lower lip down, and how your other hand is going to cradle my neck. I know how you'll smell..."

With energy I didn't know I possessed I am able to raise my brow.

"Gasoline and dark beer," she says. "But in a good way."

"Huh." My answers are limited to single syllable. All around us the day is dying. People study their watches and talk of tomorrow's five ships. The sun is setting slow, but won't go down honestly for another six weeks and will leave us for now with a funny half-assed moonlight. Real rest won't come without effort.

"Are your club members still out at the cabin?" Janey says.

For the life of me I don't know. I imagine Will and Colson, rummaging through the junk pile of my life, and want to tell them to take it all. I think of the idiots with my rifle down by the river and how even if they injure themselves the charges of negligence that are rightly mine will slide off like warming snowpack from an angled metal roof. I think of the photo in my shirt pocket and what that guy would do with this young girl in front of me. Or what he would do with me, who let him develop this soft gut over his belt and a kidney stone that keeps him hunched over in a plastic chair when we should have Janey slung across our collective shoulder and be headed for the gate. He'd find a use for the sledgehammer in his hand, if only to turn it on himself.

"No," I say. "They're gone."

Janey stretches like a foal being born, but born smiling. My pain is subsiding, enough so I can lean back without screaming.

"Mind if I grab my coat?"

I say sure and she is gone, running back into the house I saved her from. You wouldn't know the place was ever damaged, as Stuart and Vicki have dumped tons of money into renovations and additions and new paint. The basic layout remains the same, though, and I know where Janey's room is and how far she must go for her jacket.

The pain keeps me from a full speed sprint to the gate. Mine is a slumped shuffle, one last absconded beer dancing in my coat pocket. I manage a few waves and even an unnoticed smile of apology to Karen. Then I am in my truck rolling at what I hope is an inconspicuous speed up the pavement and across the bridge out of town. By the Dyea road turnoff the ache is just a humming memory, but my bladder screams the last mile. My driveway is blessedly empty of vehicles and I lock the brakes early, sliding six feet to a stop in the gravel.

Dust settles all around me as I make for the cabin, leaving the truck door open and engine idling. My front door is locked for the first time in recent memory—Colson and Will, keeping the crap of my existence safe from no one but me. I won't make the round trip to the truck for the keys, so I jump off my steps for the surrounding bushes, foraging further than necessary into the underbrush. The truck's throaty 350 is the only sound as I unbuckle and let loose. A patch of devil's club sways and bends before me and I groan like a bear with questionable intentions. The booze and blood take their sweet time and I feel good again. Afterwards, I can only pick the sturdiest birch and lean. The sun has crawled up the eastern mountains to paint the highest points of the Twin Dewey Peaks pink. I need to shut off my truck, go inside and get cleaned up and ready for work tomorrow. I need to decide what I'll do when Vicki's car with only Janey inside pulls into my driveway, if I'm going to hide or have the door open. I need to do a lot of things but end up doing nothing. I just stand and catch my breath, while behind me my blood mixes with the dirt.

Over a hundred years ago, during the Gold Rush of the 1890's, Skagway was run by a con man named Jefferson Randolph "Soapy" Smith. Maybe you've heard of him, maybe not. Soapy and his henchmen swindled the gold seekers, ran bunko games, and basically made this tent city a shitty place. The citizenry eventually hit their tipping point and formed the Committee of 101 to oust Soapy. Everything came to a head on the 8th of July when the leader of the vigilantes, Frank Reid, met Soapy down on the pier and the two shot each other in possibly the sloppiest gunfight ever. Both men died—Soapy on the spot, Reid over the next twelve days. Reid became the city's original hero. Everyone in the valley turned out for the funeral and gave him a headstone seven feet high that still reads *He gave his life for the Honor of Skagway*. Only after burying their hero did the residents find that Reid was hardly an altar boy, having fled north to avoid murder charges in Oregon. By then Reid lay safely under that cement slab chuckling up at the whole mess.

Soapy was buried about fifty feet away in a simple little plot outside the official cemetery boundary, the lone attendees of his funeral a mysterious woman, the man hired to transport the body, and a preacher who spoke only one line—"*The way of the transgressor is hard*." That was that—bible shut, body buried. Today everyone who steps off the cruise ships wants to hear about Soapy, the famous villain. At some point during the day they learn Frank Reid's name and forget it by the time they are at the midnight buffet sailing south. The bad guy became famous and the good guy got to be forgotten. I guess everything worked out.

My take on this hero bullshit is just that—it's bullshit. Sure, maybe if someone lucks out and does something special or great that they never planned on doing, give them a ride on the fire engine in the 4th of July parade or a good meal or free drinks for a week. After that, let them slide back down to wherever they began, simple and selfish and unremarkable. Let them screw up and disappoint you, and get mad at them when they do. If the rest of their existence turns out to be anything but heroic, so be it.

And ask questions. Question everything. Forget the easy standards—*How does it feel to save a life?* or *Weren't you ever concerned about your own safety?* Ask real questions, ones you might not want to ask and they don't want to answer. Ask why someone walked home from downtown on such a cold night when their truck was parked a block away and how come they took over an hour to cover only fourteen blocks. If they claim to have gone in through the window, ask why all the glass lay scattered in the snow outside. Ask how they saw a fire deep in a house thirty yards from the street they were walking on, or why a girl fleeing the house never saw them running in. Ask if they hadn't made a few off-hand comments about how Sondra was sprouting or started checking out the paperback exchange in the library where the sullen girl volunteered on Tuesdays and Wednesdays. Ask how close they thought twenty-four was to sixteen. Close enough for a hero to jump. Ask your hero what they would have done if there had been no fire.

Janey doesn't come over that night. I keep all the lights out and doors locked and consider dashing down to the river should I see headlights. But she doesn't come—not that night, not the next day or any days after that. After a week I consider calling but realize I can't think of what I would say or even readily recall Stuart and Vicki's number. I can't remember ever actually calling Janey. Since that first night our relationship has been based on stumbling into each other.

The summer rolls on, steady and unremarkable. The

season's biggest social storms—the 4th of July, Soapy's Wake and Dustball—have all blown through, trailing behind them only minor squalls that can be avoided without regret or explanation. Daylight fades a little each day and a warm drizzle moves in for the last week of July. The river and creeks swell up fat and run chocolaty grey from the hills. Upset but undeterred tourists don garbage bag ponchos to prowl the gift shops. Like most, I avoid downtown except to visit the post office and liquor store.

In early August I drive to Whitehorse where my doctor scares me with pictures of the sonar procedure that awaits me if I don't lay off the beer and sodium, dramatically up my water intake and pass the stone myself. I promise to heed his advice once south of the border, and launch one last bender while still in the Yukon. I get drunk at the 202 Motor Inn and hook up with a highway flagger girl who claims to make $50 an hour just standing out there with her STOP/SLOW sign and smells like a leather ashtray when the sun busts through the hotel blinds at four a.m. I stop twice on the way home, first to puke in the desert north of Carcross and then to pee blood into the clear water of Lake Tutshi.

My first day back at work I put in a request to switch to swing shift, telling myself and others I just need to sleep a little more. This change keeps me in the shops until eleven p.m. and gives me an excuse to stay out of the bars. All the while I keep an ear to the ground, waiting to hear something about my having abandoned Janey. Nothing comes, not from the Alder brothers, from Will or Colson or even Stuart or Vicki, who still wave when driving by on the street in a simple way that says stop by anytime. In the end I am a little surprised how easy avoiding someone is in a town barely over a mile long.

Late summer is always good for some overtime shifts so I am left with only one free day per week. My next real day off comes up shining and warm and with no excuses. Standing on my porch, drinking the first eight of my suggested daily sixty-four ounces of water, I see Skagway alive below. I want to drive down for a greasy bomb breakfast at the Sweet Tooth, maybe an early afternoon beer in the Red Onion, but I can't face the odds. Still, I've been in Southeast too long to remain indoors on a sunny day, and I soon find myself in yesterday's clothes and off the front porch, headed anywhere but towards town.

Within the hour I have walked the half-mile up the road to the Skyline trailhead and started up A.B. Mountain. The trail runs along the mountain's gradual spine for the first mile as an easy roller coaster before exploding upward onto an open rough forehead of rock outcroppings and gulleys. Sweating in my Helly Hansen jeans and work boots, I can admit myself to be winded and sadly unprepared. I stop more than a couple times to pant on the trailside and wonder aloud what the hell I am doing. I am not hiking. I know what hiking is supposed to look like, evidenced by the handful of young tan people in pocket shorts and lightweight shoes of fabric and rubber who pass me by, perspiring in an honest and natural way and asking how I'm doing with poorly-hidden real concern. Nor am I simply walking—this realization comes as the trail becomes more vertical and I climb on hands and knees through picketbrush. Sooner than expected I am above the treeline and back in the sunlight, navigating sloppy switchbacks on an incline that wants to start me rolling back down and not stop until I hit something substantial.

I neglected to bring a watch or water, but know whatever the time is I am behind on my liquid intake. Half an hour later I have found a creek fed by snow melted this morning and I cup my hands to drink. At first I try estimating the quantity of each handful and how they affect my suggested daily sixty-four ounces but soon lose count and just heave the water in. I know only that the water comes cold and delicious, and I am high above the valley I have called home since twenty-two but still somewhere I have never been before. This is as far as I can go today, so I just sit and wait for the stomach ache so much water is bound to bring.

I can't say how long I sit there. A state ferry comes into the dock, empties and fills back up with foot traffic and camper rigs before sailing south. Several small planes hug the hillside below and cut their throttles, coasting in a lazy arc back around to the runway alongside the river. The cruise ships idle with only occasional belches of horn in the harbor. Their clots of tourists pump silently through the veins of the city. Even my railroad flows seamlessly, stripped of all extraneous sounds except for the classic Baldwin steam engine dragging the parlor cars north of town to swap out with the diesels that will pull them up the pass. This illusion of a perfect place moving without noise or effort must be what makes people hike up to such heights, and what makes them want to head back down.

I fill up with creek water before starting down and stop just before dropping back into the trees, within view of everyone I know and thousands of visitors I don't, for a leak that would make my doctor happy—clear as a nun's conscience. Crawling down the steeper parts of the trail and sliding on my butt in places, I emerge onto the tamer trail dirty, sweat-soaked and bruised from a couple minor tumbles. The relatively flat path slides under my feet now, and I let gravity pick up my speed on downhill stretches. My body jiggles and bounces in places a man's should not, fighting for a pace it has never known, when finally I look down and find myself running. Honest to goodness running, like I haven't done since high school P.E. class. I laugh out loud like a loon, wondering how long this will last.

It doesn't last long, and I find myself walking the last ten minutes of trail and the stretch of road back to my cabin. The place is warm from a midday sun and takes me back in willingly. The clock reads 4:15, which I decide is either too early or late for a shower, so I refill my water jug and take my filthy self back onto the porch. Removing my boots, I pour some water over blisters I felt spooling up on my descent. They ache and though I know better something childish in me will pop them before the night is done. For now I'm going to enjoy the ache, the same way I will savor the low dull thrum in my knees and muscles tomorrow morning. From my porch I can see how far I climbed today, and how much more of the mountain waits above. I should drive down the hill for dinner. On such a beautiful night someone is surely barbequing, or maybe a good band is down from Whitehorse and playing in the Bonanza, where I could listen with Colson and an overpriced burger or find the Alder brothers to see what's happening on day shift. But I know if I descend into the city I will tell someone about today and end up outside in the street, a dumb middle-aged man pointing up at the mountain that most local kids hike before their thirteenth birthday and most adults are smart enough to stay off of altogether. All of this will be gone. I'm not ready for that. I haven't always planned well, but my cabin holds enough to keep me for tonight.

The next morning I leave early enough to swing by the Mercantile before work, parking as close as possible to the door and moving as quickly as my aching legs allow. I bypass all the slick mountaineering and camping gear for the back room. The selection of running shoes is mercifully small so my decision is easy, but the brilliant white Nikes with spring soles and spacey designs still look misplaced at the base of my work clothes.

"And these are what you want?" This from the tuque-topped clerk whose name escapes me though he's been drunk at my place several times. He grins through his goatee as I model the shoes.

"I guess," I say. "What I need."

And that's how I spend August—running. I won't call what

I am doing jogging, since to me that always signifies something healthy and pure and steady. I am just running—sometimes too fast, most times too slow. I rise every morning before work and hit the trails if the day is dry. I make my way to the Devil's Punchbowl and Sturgill's Landing and Upper Reid Falls—all places that before I could only take people's word existed. I walk when necessary and run where I can. If it's raining I head out towards Long Bay or down into town. People at first give me crazy looks or stop and ask if everything is all right and do I need a ride. Eventually word gets around because soon everyone just waves with a little smile or a patronizing thumbs-up, the kind of harmless encouragement that movies and TV tell us every lost cause deserves.

After a few weeks my midriff still bounces, but clothes hang looser and my chest looks less like boobs beneath a t-shirt. My little internal hitchhiker has made only two appearances and neither has come close to matching the pain of past episodes. I can only hope all the jumping and jostling makes him anxious to leave. I drink my water religiously and despite having to piss every half-hour can't help but feeling the effort is helping. I entertain thoughts that between the water and the running my stone will lose interest and depart without my ever noticing, disappearing into the sewers and down to the bay like a migratory bird heading south for the winter. The kind of thing where you don't even notice they are gone until you look up one morning and see only an empty sky.

A late summer heat wave drops down onto our valley as August rolls into September, overstaying its welcome and leaving the town sunburned and irritable. The Yukon stores soon sell out of fans and an old man from North Dakota off a Princess boat collapses in a gift shop, overwhelmed by humidity or scrimshaw. Prices, tips and tolerances drop daily and everyone is riding out summer's end like seniors during the last week of high school. The kids from the semester colleges started drifting south a few weeks ago, their sendoffs lost in econ season, and now the quarter school crowd trickles out every other day in ones and twos. I can't pop downtown to check my mail without some little earth muffin or GQ granola grabbing my arm and insisting I come to their going-away bash, and how they will always remember that one great blowout at my place. I promise to remember also and try to make their sendoff, lying on both fronts. I have attended that party a hundred times before and have nothing against them personally, but I will not miss them. They will return next spring and if not them, someone who looks and acts just like them, someone who likes the same bands and wants to travel to the same places next winter and thinks I'm great even though they don't really know shit about me. Like the leaves on the trees, they are pretty to look at when they bloom and would be missed if they didn't come around each year when they're supposed to, but I can't get sad when they fall off and the north wind whips them into the bay. I also know odds are Janey will be at some of these get-togethers, and eventually one will be hers. Will I be invited, and how will I weasel out if I am? Having no idea and preferring not to dwell on such things, I just keep running.

Early September finds the Transmontane Rod and Gun Club at the cabin—attendance now dwindled to Will, Colson and myself—for what we know without saying will be our last official meeting. They too will be leaving soon, but with no fanfare. Experienced seasonal drifters know better than to blast out of a summer like a rock band on a double encore. Rather, they remain quiet, like the guest who hangs around after a raging shindig just long enough to make sure everyone gets home safe and all the broken glass is swept up before slipping out with a promise to call and check on you the next morning. Will and his girlfriend are heading to the islands with spring plans no more firm than "we'll see." Colson still intends to squander his family's money on the landing craft, despite no crew and a business plan that looks worse to me with each passing week of sobriety and fading daylight. He makes one last plea which I wave off with my water bottle, then we just discuss which restaurants are still open and how many big ship days are left.

We end up watching a Discovery Channel show about smoke jumpers, those lunatics for whom tumbling out of airplanes isn't dangerous enough in its own right, so they incorporate forest fires to up the ante. Footage flashes of brave young men and women leaping feet first into Hell with little more than helmets and shovels on their backs. Most of the commentary comes from a greying fellow in crisp USFS green and eyes that know better now. He talks about up and downdrafts, crown fires where the flames ignore the ground and jump along the treetops, and the use of escape fires. This last one is a technique used when crews are retreating from a fast-moving blaze. If they come across a stretch of dry grass or similar quick burning fuel, they light the area intentionally. This new fire whips through the grass, burning itself out quickly and leaving a safe escape path, one the approaching flames will not reignite. The first recorded use of an escape fire was in 1949, the show explains, when a crew found themselves stuck in a gulch in Montana with a burn chasing them uphill. None of the fourteen smokejumpers followed the old foreman who came up with the idea. All but two died climbing toward the ridgeline. Watching this grey guy tell the story on a clear mountain afternoon in his best pressed uniform, you can see in his eyes that he doesn't know what he would have done if he had been there that day in Montana, having been both the kid who thought he was faster than fire and now the old timer. Real guts are needed to trust the thing that is trying to kill you to save your life. These escape fires are really only useful in grassy areas, the grey fellow says in closing. In the densely wooded terrain that lies outside my window, they are unlikely to help anyone.

When Will says Janey's name, I realize this is the first I have heard it aloud in over a month. My chest tingles like that first day I went up A.B. Mountain, fearful of my legs giving out and tumbling all the way back down.

"Have you talked to her recently?" Will says.

"Not in a while, I guess." I know full well I should stop right there and start talking about anything else, maybe even Colson's beer barge if necessary. "When did you see her?"

Will looks out the window, his memory tied to the setting sun on the east valley wall.

"Maybe a week ago," he says. "She was in with a couple friends. A going-away party for her friend Karen, I think."

I nod, having noticed the town a little quieter recently.

"Anyway, they were at the RO," Will says. "And she asked if you've been around and I said yeah, here and there. She heard you've been running and getting in shape and hoped everything was okay."

I acknowledge this quietly but wonder about the existence I've crafted in which exercise is viewed with equal parts admiration and suspicion.

"And she said she hadn't seen you in a while and wanted to tell you thanks," he says.

"Thanks for what?" Colson says, looking up from a 1970's issue of *Popular Mechanics* he found in a box of things my folks sent up years ago. *Build Your Own Hovercraft!* the cover promises.

"I don't know," I say. "Couldn't have been much."

"You're not out saving lives again, are you?" Colson asks.

"I'm trying not to."

"Please do." Colson drops back into *Popular Mechanics*, which brags in smaller type of light bulbs that will last your entire lifetime.

"A real gentleman," Will says.

"She said that?"

Will grins. If he wore a mustache he would be twirling the ends. "I think she even said chivalrous."

"Chivalrous?"

Colson looks up. "The whole knights and jousting and coats over puddles business?"

"I think," Will says. "The band was playing, it was hard to hear."

This is too much. With a groaning laugh, I push myself to my feet and head to the kitchen. I pull out my first beer in a month and crack the bottle open. My pointy little gut tourist has been laying low, maybe he needs something with weight to move him along. The alcohol shocks me all the way through, electrifying my teeth and spiking in my fingertips. Chivalrous. Unbelievable.

In the living room Will and Colson are at the window looking out. Fat raindrops smack into the pane and a dark cloud has rolled down the pass, looking like a sloppily-torn hole in the evening sky between the canyon walls. Soon my roof sings and the devil's club and canopy of birch trees in my yard reel from the tiny punches of the drops. The streets below swirl with pre-emptive rotors of dust in front of the storm like a kid kicking a rock down the road. Looking out to the driveway, I notice the windows on both Will's Subaru and my truck are rolled down. After weeks with no rain we have gotten spoiled. Without prompting, Will runs out to roll them all up, returning darkened in spots and chuckling.

"I think I saw some lightning." Will cranes his head against the living room glass, trying to look north of the trees outside.

"No," Colson says. "Not here."

"I've seen it here," I say. "A long time ago. A group of us were camping out at Smuggler's Cove one night, and there was a storm down by Long Falls. It was only two or three shots, but the valley lit up like a picture being made."

At least I think I saw this—the party was raging and I'd only been a hero about a year and was still enjoying the ride. Or maybe I passed out or headed to the woods with someone, and then a friend told me about the storm later. Either way, I'm confident that if I close my eyes right now I will see that lightning.

The cloud hangs over the high school, and through my wet window I can see Skagway's south end glowing in a last few minutes of sunlight. I want to call someone down there and warn them of what is coming, tell them to batten the hatches. But this little storm isn't dangerous. This is instead exactly the kind of tiny disaster from which no one wants to be saved. Sometimes we want to be caught up, have ourselves swept away and maybe just feel like we survived all on our own. Watching from the safety of my living room, I want to lace up my tennyrunners and take off into all that weather. Already I regret the beer, feeling the dark weight seeping into me. I want to sweat the alcohol out into my clothes, then be fried dry by that rare bolt of lightning, the one I may or may not have really seen so long ago.

By noon the next day I top A.B. Mountain. North of me the thinning trail continues along the mountain's rhythmic narrowing backbone, rolling along in docile humps for a few miles before mixing with competing ridgelines and erupting into a razorback of rough spires. I am confident the path only goes further, not higher. Yesterday's weather spasm blew through and I imagine everyone five thousand feet below me talking about what they were doing when they got caught in the wind and downpour and the lightning only Will saw. The storm left the night sky clear but in a hazy way that even a TV preacher would say was pretty but couldn't be fully trusted. Sure enough, a line of grey is erasing the tops of the Chilkat Mountains down the channel. That rain will set in sooner than we all think and coat this place I am standing with termination dust, reminding us the show is over and the time has come to start packing up.

Before heading out this morning I found my old paperback dictionary and looked up *chivalrous*. I had a pretty good idea what I'd find but the definition still made me angry and even now synonyms rattle between my ears like a load of firewood I forgot to tie down. *Gallant, knightly, valorous, intrepid*— all these words belong to me now, just for running from the battlefield, surrendering to a little calcium fiend when that beautiful young beast offered herself up. And I did want Janey, wanted her in that wrong way that I have wanted maybe only one other person my entire life. Hell, if the episode had been one of my lighter ones, the pain just a little less searing, I could have played through and claimed that prize earned so long ago. And I would have. Anyone who doesn't know that doesn't know who I am. But instead I ran. I should be stripped of my rank, whatever that may be, and pelted with vegetables by passersby. Fresh vegetables being the commodity they are around here, most folks would probably opt for plain old rocks, and I can't blame them.

Trudging back down the trail toward the road, I know better. The forerunner of heavier showers hits the pine and birch overhead, bigger drops getting through to me, and I see the whole matter playing out. First I saved Janey's life and now I have saved her honor, kept her pure and sweet when temptation, alcohol and guilt finally weakened her. My plan to lay low has only moved the matter along. Without my interference, this little misconception gestated into all-out horseshit. If things are left to incubate all winter, I will end up a goddamn Cary Grant in coveralls by the time the rivers flow thick with spring runoff.

Coming off the trailhead, the rain is in full swing. There's no hint of wind and drops come straight down, making the trees around me hiss on impact. For now the downpour is warm, the kind I can work outside in for days without getting a cold. I know I'm not going back to my cabin, and take a cutoff road that leads me down past the city rifle range with its beaten targets and shattered bottles before curving back along the river into the southwest corner of town.

Crossing the metal footbridge, I can see no more than a mile out into the bay and all the small planes rest quietly up at the hangar. Anything I mail this afternoon won't go out until tomorrow. I know this like I have known since starting down the mountain that this is the week of Stuart and Vicki's trip down south. Six weeks have passed since their party but I remember the dates when their beautiful daughter has the house to herself, the house that tried to eat her up, the house I can walk right into without neighbors asking any questions. These are not details a chivalrous man would remember. Mostly I know that left alone this damn world will keep chugging along on more or less the same heading like a big stable boat, swaying with the current a little, but nothing too crazy. If you really want to screw something up—like sending that boat right into the rocks—you have to get your hands dirty and do things yourself.

The door opens and there stands Vicki, wearing a soft workout suit that might be trendy on someone a generation younger.

"Randall." This comes like she just found a ten-spot in a jacket pocket.

"Hey, Vicki." I am one year her junior, but feel all of twelve standing on her porch. "Weren't you guys going to Seattle?"

"Stuart's there now," Vicki says. "I just didn't feel like spending money on airfare to sit around or go shopping while he was in meetings. Going Outside just doesn't have the draw it used to."

Inside the television mumbles with some syndicated sitcom we've both seen a hundred times.

"Janey isn't around, is she?"

Vicki says no, Janey went to Whitehorse for the day with Chad, whom I can only assume is the Hitler Youth from the croquet match.

"He's been fawning over her all summer," Vicki says. "I guess she just felt some pity and took him along to get some groceries and see what's playing at the movies."

I nod in understanding. Vicki peers at my wet clothes and past me at the rain, as if noticing this all for the first time.

"It's pouring, Randall, and you're soaked. Why don't you come in for a minute?"

As I step inside, she wrings out the hood of my sweatshirt onto the linoleum around me. "I would think you'd have sense enough to stay in out of this weather."

I can't make eye contact with Vicki, but I can smile.

"Yeah, you'd think."

I guess people have always needed heroes, even though very few of us ever want to be truly saved. Maybe heroes are necessary to show us all what we could do or be if we just applied ourselves and how there's something special inside everyone and all that shiny Disney-ending bullshit. But then I see Bruce Willis saving a building with no shoes on or some eighty-pound girl winning the Olympics on a sprained ankle and I feel a million miles away. I don't care how many times they go on *Oprah* or get on the cover of *People* and spout crap about how they're like anyone else—there is just no bridging that gap. We even revel in their fuckups. When they get caught screwing the wrong person or driving drunk in their BMW or punching a photographer, the incident is blown up into a marquee production on fifty of my satellite's two hundred channels. And the TV hosts talk about how this hero's new spouse—invariably their third or fourth—is their true love or how brave they are for overcoming their drug of choice for yet another time. We eat it up. Somehow we go on believing this person will come back to score the game-winning, fall-away jumper or save us from that rogue meteorite or a bus that can't slow down, or maybe even from our own burning house.

Have you ever stopped to think that maybe these indiscretions aren't accidents, but rather subconscious actions, actions that even the people committing them don't realize they are doing intentionally? Maybe they can convince themselves, as they hope to do with us, these are acts of youthful indiscretion or a wild streak due to newfound wealth and fame, when in reality they know somewhere down in the marrow of their heroic bones that they can't keep up their own sad front. They need to sink to their natural level with all of us, and every time they screw up and come out smelling like homemade cinnamon rolls is another time they must start the process all over again. As to why do they do this, I can offer only one pseudo-hero's insight. Maybe they just want us to know they won't be there for us. Maybe they are saying if you get a chance to save a life, make it your own.

If I hadn't known the layout of Vicki's house perfectly, I probably would have puked all over her new carpet. But I know the main bathroom is just outside her bedroom, first door on the left and offset slightly from Janey's room. I am slowed only by my body itself, tightening like a wet ball of paper towels around the rising sun in my pelvis. I know there is a fancier facility in her master bedroom, but despite this afternoon's other activities, throwing up in Stuart's personal clean toilet would feel intrusive.

I take time to lock the door behind me and drop to my knees in front of the bowl, letting loose a watery mix of energy bars and last night's Doritos binge. The Canuck doctor had said the pain might get this bad, some women comparing the ordeal to childbirth, but the nausea has until now remained mild and rarely come to fruition. This is new, and I get one strong shot out before dry heaving, trying to dislodge the fiery shard bouncing inside. I am suddenly aware of my own moans echoing in the shiny porcelain bowl.

Vicki is at the door. "Randall? Are you okay?"

I grunt a reply meant to sound like "Yeah, fine," but surely haven't fooled her. Vicki says okay all soft and friendly, like that sweat suit she was wearing when she invited me inside earlier. I had commented that the outfit looked good on her and she'd laughed, saying how Janey found the outfit in a closet and insisted that it was back in style now. Vicki had made some funny comment about how an article of clothing probably only qualifies as retro if you didn't wear it the first time around. I responded about how the world seems to be looping back every twenty years and coming up from behind to get us, though I wasn't sure if this was good or bad. Things hadn't taken too long after that.

The sharper edges are coming off the ache and I can rear back on my knees, wishing I could hide from the reflection in the full-wall mirror. Why in the world would someone think their guests want to watch themselves on the crapper? Staring back is a man older than I am. His shoulders and chest are thin from a recent exercise binge, in spite of which a small soft belly remains. Ribs are visible during deeper breaths, though not in a good way, and his skin is the white of cheap bread only kids eat. The flat light coming in from this grey afternoon does him no favors and we both know this body has gotten farther than it deserves.

Again, Vicki. "Are you sure I can't do anything?"

"I'm good," I say. "Just need a minute."

Standing is no small feat, my stomach still feeling like it is held at some fixed point in space by tight wires shooting off in six different directions, every movement tugging them just so slightly. I pull myself up using porcelain, towel rods and faucet handles, rising like a proud caveman and letting go into the toilet. That little bastard is on the move. I scream once or twice, my lips attempting to muffle them but doing no real good at all. In the edge of my vision the skinny fat man is whimpering, legs shaking under the weight of a tiny chunk of crystal. I don't know how to tell him that he has somehow earned all of this.

Even over my own sounds and Vicki whimpering at the door, I swear I hear that thing rebound off the bowl and into the water. My stomach winds down like a jet engine and soon I own my breath again. Clearing my eyes of tears, I look for evidence. I want to see this little devil who lived rent-free, trashed the place and ruined my summer. He is gone, though, somewhere in the murkiness below or perhaps already rolling down the pipes and southbound towards to the bay. Like a March chill after a warm February, life shoots back through me. No Canadian laser show will be taking place in my soft midsection. I can ingest all the soda and beer and sodium my system can take, and stop pouring water down my throat like a man bent on drowning himself on dry land.

I start laughing. The guy next to me in the mirror does too, causing us both to laugh that much more. Something has changed. Maybe the quality of light coming in or this new stance lessens his paunch and spreads his shoulders a little wider. His chuckling form seems much more appealing. On closer inspection, all that exercise and trekking the trails and water drinking have helped. He isn't the prettiest specimen you will see today, but who wouldn't want to kill a few hours with this fellow?

"Randall?"

Vicki. I flush the toilet and rinse with mouthwash before opening the door as if this episode is standard post-coital procedure. Her form is contained in a thick terrycloth bathrobe, ample enough to absorb a small lake. To her credit, the aerobics classes have served Vicki well even if gravity is straightening a few curves. Her earlier moves were those of a veteran shortstop fighting to keeping their starting spot. The swatch of shoulder she hasn't covered reminds me my life is my own again, and my life includes the rest of the afternoon.

"So," I say. "Where were we?"

"What the hell was that?" She looks me up and down, unarguably her right.

"Just kind of a minor medical issue. Everything is cool now." My thumb finds her chin and I lean in. "I'll explain later. After."

She grimaces, her better judgment tested for the second time today. I lean into her neck, tightening my throat in preparation for an "Ah, baby," to make Prine himself jealous.

"Randall," she says. "I think the kids are back."

Once again I am out the window. No little girl in my arms this time, just my running shoes and hooded sweatshirt, warm from a turn in Vicki's dryer during our tryst. My socks hit Stuart's thick lawn, which will remain lush and green all winter, and soak through in seconds. The downpour has not let up but is still better than the snow I hit with Janey years back. Inside Vicki is concocting a story I suggested about a flu overtaking her quickly and keeping her in bed all day, stalling Janey and the beefsteak in the front room so I can have the backyard and alley for escape.

My sweatshirt slips on like a used towel and I head to the gate. My first shoe seats quickly despite still being tied, but the second sends me to my ass on the edge of the lawn. My hands are slick with rain and grass and the damn shoe doesn't think it can fit around my wet sock. Only in grunting against the sloppy Nike do I realize how much of my energy that damn stone dragged down the toilet. I could have dropped back on Stuart's beautiful turf and gone to sleep the rest of the afternoon, soaking in all that water I no longer needed.

Looking up, there stands Chad. His clothes are a study in preplanned messiness, and his hair is just wet enough to look really good and isn't getting any wetter. The raindrops seem to fall around him. On each shoulder is a bag of Scotts Weed & Feed. This is Stuart's secret—he swears by the stuff, which he gets for a steal at a Whitehorse store whose name he's reluctant to share.

"How was the big city?" I say.

Chad shrugs, his shoulders not even noticing the fertilizer's weight.

"Okay, I guess."

My foot now slips easily into the shoe with a wet sucking sound. I stand, my sweatpants soaked an incriminating color guaranteeing I'll be offered no rides on my walk home. I point out Stuart's small storage shed across the yard. The shed's tidy paint and trim matches the house perfectly.

"Those bags go in there, opposite the garden tools."

He looks at the shed, then back to me.

"Did you bring anything back from Tim Hortons?" I say.

He shakes his head. "We ate at Dairy Queen, and brought back some KFC for Janey's mom."

"And you didn't stay for a movie?"

"Nothing good was playing."

"Still," I say. "You make the drive, might as well stay and see something."

Unsure of my logic, Chad readjusts the bags and starts to the shed.

"Well, mister," he says. "I better put these away."

I should be angry about the *mister*, but dismiss the designation as badly-aimed manners and start down the alley.

"Sure," I say. "Have a good winter."

Things are going to happen now. We are late in the season,

but there's time enough for something to drop in over the city like a freezing fog until Halloween, not particularly dangerous but keeping people indoors. Or maybe this will fall like the heavy shit-rain the valley needs and no one can ignore. I make a note to get my serious banking done in the next day or two, before Stuart returns. Maybe I should take all my savings out of the city limits and bury the money in coffee cans around my property. I should worry what people will think, how old Randall finally went too far this time. I should worry about the unreturned waves and clipped conversations at the post office that await me as this mile-long town shrinks even more below my porch. But my biggest fear is meek Stuart coming back and doing nothing, accepting all this like the inevitability it felt like to Vicki and I an hour ago. Janey will disappear to school and write a vacant card around Christmas, mentioning only the rigors of grad school and how she can't wait for next summer. And Vicki will continue smiling hello at basketball games and inviting me to Thanksgiving or Christmas dinner, though maybe now leaving a note on my door or under my truck's windshield wiper instead of risking a phone call.

Whatever happens, I welcome it. Maybe I will stay holed up in my cabin and watch everything unfold below like yesterday's crazy thunderstorm. Or maybe I'll be somewhere in British Columbia on Colson's drunk boat, sailing against the tide of reason. Maybe I'll make a trip down south and visit some art galleries, inquiring about any work they might have by Sondra. I imagine her as being very successful though reclusive, and a little detective work on my part will be necessary to find her home with a studio in the back. In my mind everything about her place is damp, the property sitting on or near the water and overly prone to rain even by Pacific Northwest standards. Any fire that erupts won't last long. I will walk right up to the front door and knock, taking advantage of her wordless surprise to tell her how everything worked itself out. She will be thirty-six and, because we are now even, maybe ready to start with a clean slate. I have time to think about all this on my walk home. Looking up, the mountain I was on top of only hours ago is gone beneath ill-defined clouds. This will be a wet walk, and a true walk for sure. I'm through running for now.

At the alley's end, I know if I turn back Chad will be looking at me—maybe over the fence or from the shed or just slackjawed from our meeting point on the lawn's edge. I don't look because I can hear those synapses firing even through this downpour. He may need to sit down and write some notes or sketch the whole thing out, but will eventually put all the pegs in the right holes. If I knew him a little better I might ask or simply expect the kid to remain silent due to some unspoken code. He will tell Janey, though, tell her everything he know or thinks he knows or maybe more. He doesn't know what else to do. And he wants to and has no reason not to. He doesn't know me or owe me anything. To him, I am nobody.

Marcel Jolley was born in Skagway, Alaska, and now lives in Camas, Washington, with his wife and son. His story collection *Neither Here Nor There* (Black Lawrence Press, 2007) won the inaugural St. Lawrence Book Award.